GO NOT GENTLY

Juggling the school run with private investigating, Sal Kilkenny's life is a strange mix of the dramatic with the domestic. Sal has two new clients: Jimmy Achebe wants her to confirm his suspicions of his wife's infidelity, while Agnes Donlan fears for her friend Lily, who has undergone a swift decline in her nursing home. Sal soon finds herself in treacherous territory which threatens to impinge on her private life...

GO NOT GENTLY

by

Cath Staincliffe

Magna Large Print Books
Long Preston, North Yorkshire,
BD23 4ND, England.

British Library Cataloguing in Publication Data.

Staincliffe, Cath
    Go not gently.

    A catalogue record of this book is
    available from the British Library

    ISBN   978-0-7505-3838-1

First published by Headline Book Publishing,
a division of Hodder Headline PLC, 1997

This edition first published in United Kingdom by C&R Crime,
an imprint of Constable & Robinson Ltd., 2013

Copyright © Cath Staincliffe, 1997

Cover illustration © David Ridley by arrangement with
Arcangel Images Ltd.

Published in Large Print 2014 by arrangement with
Constable & Robinson Ltd.

Magna Large Print is an imprint of Library Magna Books Ltd.

Printed and bound in Great Britain by
T.J. (International) Ltd., Cornwall, PL28 8RW

In loving memory – Edith Lund, Ethel Lund,
Annie Staincliffe and Flo Staincliffe

Thank you to all the people who helped me to write this book: to Dr Debra Bradley, Peter Parish MD, Lavinia Payne and Dr Mark Perry, for answering my particular scientific and medical queries; to the novel-writing group, Christina, Maggie, Marion and Natasha, for support, criticism and hugely enjoyable discussions; to all the readers who asked how I was getting on; and to Mike for solving the various mysteries that my computer dreams up.

CHAPTER ONE

'I'm concerned about her,' she was saying, 'she's so...' the patina of lines on her face creased into a frown as she groped for the word she wanted, 'distant. She's losing interest.' Her voice rose in agitation. 'It's not like Lily.'

Agnes Donlan was beautiful. And very old. Clean, airy white hair framed her face. Not the sort of colour you could get out of a bottle. White teeth too, very even, probably not her own.

'How long has she been there?' I pulled my notebook closer to jot things down.

'Eight weeks. She had the bad fall at the beginning of October and she was in the week before Christmas. It was all such a rush. She'd made up her mind. I was against it. Once you leave your own home, your independence...' She left the sentence hanging, its implication clear.

'So her decline could well be due to the move?'

Agnes fiddled with the jet brooch on her

coat. 'Oh, I don't know. If that was it, then, well,' she spread her hands, palms up, 'I'd just have to accept it, but...'

She couldn't bring herself to say it aloud.

'Listen, Miss Donlan.' I leant back and made eye contact. Her eyes were a deep blue, almost navy, like her coat. 'If I'm to help I need to know exactly what's worrying you. What you'd like me to do.'

'It sounds so melodramatic,' she protested.

I smiled. 'Everything between us is completely confidential. If I think the case is ridiculous, a waste of my time and your money, I'll say so.'

'Good. It's so hard to know.' She took a breath and straightened up in the chair. 'Very well. I'm concerned,' she spoke slowly, choosing her words with care, 'that Lily's health is being affected, that something in that place is making her ill.' Her composure wobbled as she voiced her fears, and tears glistened in her eyes. She blinked them away. 'It sounds far-fetched, doesn't it?'

'No. You may be right. We'd need to find out about conditions there, try to discover whether there's anything practical that can be done to improve her care. Sort out whether it's the upset of moving that's unsettled her or something else. Has Mrs Palmer got a

12

social worker?'

Agnes nodded. 'There was someone helped with the move, I think. The doctor sent them.'

'Well, perhaps you can talk to them first.'

'Oh, I don't feel I can, you see. I did talk to Mrs Knight, she's the matron. She said we just had to accept it, she said Lily was starting with Alzheimer's or something similar.'

'But you're not sure?'

'It's been so sudden. Everything I've read or heard suggests it comes on gradually. I can't just leave it like this. I feel I owe it to Lily to do something.'

I nodded. Considered what she'd said. Perhaps this visit to me was her way of refusing to face reality. Her reluctance to accept her friend's rapid decline. Without further investigation it was hard to make a judgement.

I suggested to Agnes that we arrange a visit to Homelea once I'd done a little research to establish whether Lily's symptoms were par for the course. The initial visit would be free of charge and afterwards I would advise her whether to retain my services or not. She agreed and thanked me, relief relaxing her shoulders as she sat back in the chair.

'All right,' I said, 'I'll need to write down all the facts we've got.'

Twenty minutes later I followed Agnes up the stairs to the ground floor. I rent office space in the cellar of the Dobsons' family home, round the corner from my own house. When I first set up business, I went knocking on neighbours' doors to find a room; the Dobsons were happy to take me in and it's worked out well. It's basic accommodation, to say the least, but I pay a peppercorn rent for it, which is all my irregular income runs to.

She got a plastic rain hood from her bag. I opened the door. She tilted her head at the steady drizzle. 'They forecast rain.' She tied the hood under her chin. 'Thank you.' She pulled on her gloves.

'Bye-bye,' I replied. 'I'll be in touch later in the week and we can arrange that visit.'

I watched while she made her way down the path and along the street, her pace slow but assured. When she reached the corner she turned a little stiffly and raised her hand in farewell. I waved back and went in.

Down in the cellar I put the kettle on and recapped on the notes I'd made. Lily Palmer had been in Homelea Private Residential Nursing Home for two months. In that time, to quote her friend Agnes, 'The life had gone out of her'. She'd lost weight, interest and seemed disoriented. She'd complained of headaches and palpitations. Sometimes she was drowsy and unresponsive, at others agitated, restless. She was often confused and forgetful.

When Agnes expressed her concern to Mrs Knight, the matron, she was invited in for a chat with Mrs Valley-Brown, the manager. Mrs Valley-Brown and her husband ran Homelea.

Matron took care of nursing those residents who needed it. Mrs Valley-Brown told Agnes that Lily had Alzheimer's and that the doctor had prescribed a tranquilliser to help calm her down. If she responded well to the medication her behaviour would settle down, she'd be less distressed. They also had sleeping pills they could administer when needed as Lily had begun to suffer from insomnia, restlessness and occasional night incontinence. Lily was welcome to stay at Homelea as long as her behaviour didn't adversely affect the other residents.

The kettle clicked off and I made myself a coffee, took it over to my desk. There'd been something a little strange at that point in the interview. I'd asked Agnes what would happen if Lily got much worse. Her hand flew to

15

the jet brooch on her coat and she'd squeezed it tight. Otherwise, she completely ignored my question. A pause and then she began talking about Lily's marriage. Something in my question had frightened Agnes. Fear of the death that might follow or the thought of increasing frailty? Whatever it was, I hadn't got an answer.

I skimmed the rest of my notes. Lily had married, had a son and daughter. The girl had died in childhood but Charles lived down in Devon, visited twice a year, wrote monthly. He'd helped sort out the move to Homelea. Lily's husband, George, had gone missing in action in the Far East in 1944. Once Charles left home Lily had worked as a secretary and book-keeper for a small firm. Since retirement she'd been fit and active. She'd fallen twice at home, fractured her wrist the first time and dislocated her shoulder the second. The move to Homelea had been at her own instigation. Apart from the shoulder and a certain nervousness about falling, Lily had been fit as a fiddle when she left her own house for Homelea. There had been no sign of mental frailty then.

Eight weeks.

I tilted my chair back dangerously and made a survey of my office while I let the information trickle round my brain. The blind over the basement window was broken. Roller blinds are about as reliable as flip-top bins. The year planner that I'd put up the previous January in the hope it'd help me plan my time was still blank apart from school holidays. My sort of work doesn't get planned. It's all response and reaction. Go here, do this, try that, meet so-and-so.

The rest of the room was dusty but reasonably neat, shabby carpet, painted filing cabinet, a set of three dining chairs. A stack of reference books on a shelf, phone and answerphone, a pretty ceramic plate wall clock the only personal touch.

I tidied up the desk, switched the answerphone on and prepared to leave. I was at the Dobsons' front door when I heard my office phone. I clattered down the stairs, flung myself at the desk and yanked the answer-phone connection out of the socket, interrupting my recorded voice in mid-greeting. Pressing the off button never does any good; it's one of those slow response – maybe I'll do it this time maybe I won't – models.

'Hello. Sal Kilkenny Investigations, Sal Kilkenny speaking.'

'Oh.' Confusion at the other end of the line. 'Erm, I just thought...' Laugh. Young, male, nervous. Either the answerphone, or the fact that I was a woman, had thrown him. Most people think Sal's a man. My Yellow Pages ad is carefully worded. It says female detectives available but doesn't imply it's a one-woman show. No point in advertising for abusive calls and attracting all the headcases.

More nervous laughter.

'How can I help?' Not 'Can I?' but 'How can I?' Make the client confident you can do the job.

'Well, it's my wife. Do you ... look, I've never ... I haven't any idea what you charge or even if...'

Wish he'd spit it out. 'I can offer an initial appointment, no obligation. You can discuss the matter with us, find out the sort of services we can offer and take it from there. Or I can offer free advice now if you want to talk about it over the phone.'

'I see. Erm ... well. Oh, shit, sorry.' He hung up. Caught in the act, I'd guess.

I plugged in the answerphone again, hoping it wouldn't take revenge at sudden disconnection by playing up and taking half-messages again, refusing to playback or to play the announcement, confusing people with uncomfortable silences and sequences of beeps. I sometimes spent hours searching for fragments of communication, whizzing the tape back and forth. I suppose the answerphone matched the window blind really. Crap. And not a true reflection of the quality of work I could offer.

Positive thinking.

After all, two clients in one day can't be bad, even if one did ring off.

CHAPTER TWO

The drizzle looked set to run for days, the sky was dense and sullen. I did my best to ignore it as I walked up to school to collect Maddie and Tom.

'We had wet play again,' Maddie complained. 'I hate wet play.'

'But you play inside, don't you? Games and things?'

'No we don't,' she said scornfully. 'We do drawing or read a book.' On a par with waiting for a bus by the sound of it.

'Hold this.' She thrust her lunch box, book bag and PE things at me.

Maddie was always the pits after school.

I turned to Tom, who was wrestling with

his coat, and sorted him out.

'We did puppets.' He held up a navy sock with felt eyes and ears glued on to it. The ears were triangular. There were no other distinguishing features.

'Is it a cat?'

'No,' he grinned, 'it's a sock monster.' Of course.

'Come on,' Maddie yelled, 'I'm getting soaking here.'

We were all soaked by the time we got back. I hung clothes on radiators to steam and provided warm drinks and crumpets. I left the kids with theirs in front of the telly while I went to chop vegetables: carrots, onions, turnips, beans. We've a big kitchen – the whole house is big, a Victorian semi, red-brick and stained glass. But originally there'd been a dining room and a scullery-size kitchen. The owner of the house had knocked the two together. In the centre there's a huge oval table, soft light wood. Ray made it. His pride and joy. I seem to spend half my life at that table. Sun streams in the kitchen most of the day in the summer. In mid-February it doesn't. I drew the blinds and turned on the lamps and lights.

A gentle snore from under the table told

me Digger the dog was still alive. I returned to my chopping and sifted through people I could usefully talk to about Lily Palmer before I went to see Homelea for myself. I came up with two. I set some of the vegetables to simmer and tried the phone.

Rachel, the social worker who was a friend of a friend, was away on a training day. I dialled the other number.

Moira answered the phone with the same brusque voice that had alienated so many potential patients. Those who'd stuck it out beyond first impressions discovered a dedicated GP with a genuine concern for their wellbeing. She'd a healthy mistrust of drug companies and unnecessary medical intervention. She often referred people to alternative therapies, sent them off to the homeopathic clinic in Manchester or to try acupuncture. She was not popular with the medical establishment. Her surgery was always full to bursting. She never bothered with appointments, her method of actually listening to people and giving them space to talk put paid to any notion of time management. We didn't mind waiting. It was worth it.

'Sal,' she barked, 'how are you? Well?'

'I'd like a chat. I need to do a bit of research for a case I'm working on. When are you free?'

'I'm on call tonight, that do you?'

'Fine. It shouldn't take that long.'

'Half-eight?'

'Yes.'

I knew that could mean any time from half-eight till half-eleven. Moira always intended to be on time and made precise arrangements, never acknowledging that the demands of her practice frequently played havoc with her social plans.

'Need any books? What's the general area?'

'Geriatrics, Alzheimer's, that sort of thing.'

'OK.'

'Oh, and drugs, stuff about side effects.'

'Hah!' she snorted. 'Give me a few weeks. Later.'

'Later' was Moira's version of goodbye.

I fried onion, cumin and ginger, chilli, coriander and turmeric. While the spices sizzled I set the table. I added the veg and a tin of tomatoes to the pan and stirred the lot. Left it to cook.

Ray got in just as I was draining the rice. Digger emerged from under the table and went apeshit for a few minutes. Ray joined in. Prancing about and grabbing folds of the dog's loose coat and wriggling it about, letting the animal lap at his moustache with his broad pink tongue. Greeting ritual over, Digger slunk back under the table.

'It's ready,' I said. 'Tell the kids.'

Teatime was relatively peaceful, an inkling of what might emerge as the kids matured. But at five and four respectively, Maddie and Tom were still barely civilised at the table. All too often food became an area for defiance. I'd long since given up trying to get Maddie to eat a balanced diet. As long as she treated what was on the plate as something to eat rather than modelling clay, ammunition or paint I was happy.

Ray takes the same tack with Tom. We're both single parents and we have to agree on ground rules for the kids to avoid their playing us off against each other. Ray and I share the house and the childcare but never a bed. Some people seem to find it hard to believe; I don't know whether it's the shared child-care or the asexual relationship that gives them the most trouble. It's the latter as far as Ray's mother is concerned. She thinks we're lying about it.

By eight o'clock the children were asleep, the pots washed and the kitchen clear. I sat in the old overstuffed armchair by the bay window, feet up on a chair, and browsed through the evening paper. 'Council Freezes Repairs', 'Triple Wedding at Hacienda', 'School Will Sell Land', 'Man Held in Shooting'. My head nodded as I settled in. I jerked awake to the sound of the doorbell. Quarter to nine. Not bad.

Moira's tall, spindly frame filled the doorway. She came in hugging her doctor's case and a Tesco carrier bag, and followed me through into the kitchen.

'God, it's years,' she boomed, looking round.

'Still the same,' I said. 'Besides, you're always too busy and I've sort of lost the habit of inviting people round to eat.'

'Should do it again,' she admonished. 'Social eating relieves stress.'

'Depends who you do it with,' I thought of the children, 'and who's cooking. What about Christmas dinner? That's pretty stressful if you're the one with the turkey.'

'Family don't count.' She grinned, took off her jacket and scarf and draped them over one of the chairs. Pulled out another one and sat down. 'Well?'

I explained to Moira the basic facts about Lily Palmer's decline. Her fall, the dislocated shoulder, her move to Homelea and

24

the change in her behaviour, the confusion, the loss of sparkle. How could I establish whether she was being treated competently?

'Difficult. Find out what medication she's on, the drugs and the dosage. People give bucketloads sometimes. Any of the things you mention could be side effects. See the GP. Ask for a diagnosis. What she first presented with, chronology of symptoms. Alzheimer's, pre-dementia.' She puffed her cheeks out with air then slowly released it. 'Whole other ball game. There can be confusion after trauma – the fall, the move. Should have regained equilibrium by now. Two months?'

'Yes.' I picked a satsuma from the bowl. 'Two since she moved, four since the fall.'

'Don't do anything drastic,' Moira continued, 'no sudden stop on medication. Who's treating her? Own GP?'

'I don't know. Her friend said there was a matron at the home who ran the nursing side.'

'She wouldn't prescribe. But once she'd got something from the doctor she could reorder easily enough. Some people go on for years on drugs they should only have had for a couple of weeks.'

'What about the dosages, if–'

Before I could finish, Moira's bleeper sounded. She switched it off and went to use the phone in the hall.

'Woman in labour.' She scooped up her jacket and case. 'Every time I cover for Dr Wardle one of his mothers gets going. Have a look at these,' she pushed the Tesco carrier across the table, 'couple of years old. Most of it's still relevant. Must go. Later. Ring me.'

I saw her out, watching as she folded herself into the little Fiat she drove.

Two of the books were on geriatric medicine, one of those covered mental health in particular. The other, Medicines, was a family guide. It listed common drugs and what they were used for, and each entry included all of the side effects that could occur. Enough to put anybody off rushing out to buy all those over-the-counter drugs advertised on the telly.

I made a cup of tea and joined Ray in the lounge. He was sprawled on the sofa watching the news. Toys were still scattered about, and plates with remains of crumpets.

'Home visit?' he asked.

'No, picking her brains. I've got a new case needing a bit of medical background. You know you've still got paint in your hair.'

'Where?' He ran his hands over his dark

26

springy curls.

'There, at the front.'

He stood up and peered in the mirror. 'I told them not to start the painting yet. It'll only need doing again, there's that much dust flying around.' He smoothed his moustache. 'But they're in such a hurry. Bonuses for bringing it in by the end of March.' In between making his own wooden furniture to order Ray took on sub-contract work with a couple of builders.

He bared his teeth, turned his profile this way and that.

'Ray!'

'What?'

'Preening.'

'Just checking.'

'What? That there's no paint on your teeth. You're just vain.'

'No. Careful with my appearance. It's in my blood, style, all Italians have it. You English have no idea.'

'Yeah, yeah, yeah.'

He turned back to the mirror to smooth his hair again. Bit pointless. Then whistled the dog. Digger came bounding in, Ray did something playful to his ears and the two of them went off for walkies.

I put Moira's books on one side then

swept toys into one corner of the room where I couldn't actually see them from the sofa. I removed crumpets and crockery. There was nothing worth watching on television so I watched nothing for half an hour. My yawning reached chronic proportions.

In bed I guzzled a couple of chapters of my library book. When the print began to blur I switched out the lamp and hugged the duvet to me.

I could hear the dog down the street yapping. On and on. I felt my shoulders tense with irritation. Noise pollution. Why couldn't they just let the creature in or remove its vocal cords? I'd time it tonight. Begin to gather hard facts so I could challenge the neighbours. See how long it kept me awake. It was too much effort to lift my head up to read the clock. I fell asleep.

CHAPTER THREE

I rang Rachel, my social work contact, at ten a.m. She was busy for the rest of the day: visits, case conference, court reports, the lot. After further prodding and a promise to foot the bill I persuaded her to meet me for lunch the following day. Her office is in Longsight, mine in Withington. We agreed on a friendly Greek restaurant in Fallowfield, midway between us.

I stuck some washing in the machine, then sat in the kitchen and browsed through the books that Moira had left. It became clear that dementia wouldn't have resulted from either Lily's fall or from leaving her home. But both the books listed two types of dementia, Alzheimer's and something called acute confusional disorder. The latter could result from physical illness, like a severe infection or as a reaction to drugs. So it could be treated and would stop, unlike actual senile dementia.

Agnes had described Lily's decline as rapid, the books said Alzheimer's developed slowly over several months. But Mrs Valley-Brown had told Agnes that Lily had Alzheimer's disease, the commonest form of dementia. Presumably the GP knew how to tell the two states apart and for some reason they'd discounted acute confusion. I understood Agnes' disquiet: at first glance the facts didn't appear to add up.

I opened my notepad and listed the questions we needed answers to. The more I thought about it the more likely it seemed that there'd been a misdiagnosis. That an untreated illness or an adverse reaction to medication had led to Lily Palmer becoming troubled, confused, unlike her usual self. If we could establish the cause and treat it then Lily would get better and Agnes would have her old friend back. It wasn't right: Agnes had been anxious enough to come to a private investigator when the Homelea staff dismissed her concerns. They should have been on to it straight away.

I switched the washing to the tumble dryer in the cellar, then made a quick foray to the shops on my bicycle. Withington is a real mix of taste and tack. Discount shops selling brightly coloured, semi-disposable goods made in China and the Philippines nestle cheek by jowl with more upmarket outlets: delicatessens, health-food shop, designer clothes boutiques.

I bought pasta, cheese and milk from the small supermarket, then negotiated my way to the greengrocer's. The pavements were narrow and crowded with shoppers. I wheeled my bike along the gutter to avoid colliding with anyone.

I was tempted by gleaming displays of avocados, imported beef tomatoes, limes and grapes, by bright bunches of hothouse herbs, but I resisted. Our budget rarely ran to the exotic end of the stall. If it was in season or on offer we ate it. Cabbage, carrots, turnips, onions. Fruit was the exception as the mainstay of the battle against tooth decay: 'No you can't, have some fruit.'

It had actually stopped raining but the cold, grey fug lingered as though the drizzle had been freeze-framed. Back home I had cheese on toast, pulled on another sweater and gathered things up to take round to the office.

The crocuses that dotted gardens along the way had taken a battering from the recent gales. The purple and yellow flowers lay sprawled and broken. I'd never bothered with crocuses, they were just too feeble for the season. I stuck to polyanthus and primroses, snowdrops and winter pansies – lovely gaudy colours for murky winter days.

I picked up my business mail from the table in the hall and went down to the cellar. The answerphone light blinked three times and paused. I hung my coat on the back of the door and made ready to take notes. The first message was from Wondawindow Systems, from Michelle, no less, who would call again later to discuss with me the new range of low-maintenance, high-quality, fully guaranteed, top-security, bonus-offer uPVC double-glazed windows currently available. I glanced at the narrow basement window with its broken blind. Shrugged.

The second caller had rung off without leaving a message. The third was the man who'd rung me the previous afternoon. I recognised the nervous laugh.

'Hello...' laugh. 'Yeah, it's about something I want you to investigate. Can you ring me at work?' He reeled off the number. 'And, erm...' laugh, 'if I'm out on a job then leave a message for me and I'll ring you when I get back. Right.' Pause. 'Thanks.'

Well, I'd have done so gladly but he hadn't left his name. I did try the number on the off chance it was a direct line. A woman answered. 'Hello, Swift Deliveries.'

I explained that I wanted to get in touch with one of the younger men whose name I'd forgotten. She couldn't help.

'We've fifteen drivers, love. All over the region. I need a name.'

I gave up. With luck, he'd try again.

My mail consisted of bumf from the bank trying to get me to take out a loan and a letter from the accountants asking for my detailed income and expenditure so they could prepare my year-end accounts.

I spent the rest of the afternoon preparing my accounts. It would have been easier if I'd entered things on a more regular basis but I shoved all my invoices and receipts into a box file marked 'Finance' and left it till the dreaded letter arrived. It wasn't even all that complicated. The thought of doing it was always worse than the reality.

By the time I'd finished I reckoned I'd have to pay about £500 tax in a couple of instalments over the next year. I couldn't believe that I could earn so little and still have to pay tax. I certainly didn't have a spare £500 sloshing round in the bank. Oh, well. It wasn't due yet and maybe by the time that bill came in I'd have found a nice little earner.

The phone interrupted my musing.

'Hello, is that Miss Kilkenny?'

'Yes. Miss Donlan?'

'That's right. I was wondering how you were getting along.' She spoke tentatively, she didn't want to bother me but she was worrying herself sick.

'Fine. I've been doing a bit of background reading and talking to people. I didn't want to visit Mrs Palmer until I'd a little more information. But we could fix that up now.'

'Yes.'

'How about Friday?'

'Oh.' A note of disappointment.

Did she want to go tomorrow? I was meeting Rachel for lunch but that left gaps either end of the day. And I couldn't see it mattered which order I did things in. 'Unless you want to go tomorrow.'

'I'd like that.'

'Does it matter when? Are there visiting times?'

'Oh no. We can visit whenever we like. I wouldn't want you to get the wrong impression. It's quite a nice place really, comfortable.'

'How about half-past ten? I could come and pick you up.'

'I'll get the bus.'

'I think it'll look better if we arrive together. If it's no trouble.'

'Of course, yes.'

I checked her address and arranged to pick her up a little before ten thirty the following morning.

No sooner had I put the phone down than it rang again.

'Hello. This is Michelle from Wondawindow Systems. We have some very attractive special offers on at the moment. I'd like to arrange a convenient time for our rep to call on you, at your own convenience, without any obligation, to discuss options with you.' Her voice was brisk, cheery and full of laboured reassurance.

'No thanks.' I got it in quickly, but she hardly drew breath.

'The Wondawindows System not only improves security and reduces maintenance but can dramatically cut heating costs and increase the value of your property.'

'No.'

'Have you thought about window improvements?'

'No. I–'

'There'd be no obligation.'

'I'm not interested.' I put the phone down before she had a chance to carry on. The things some people do for a living.

Ray was working on a conversion job (old houses to new sheltered flats). He was doing all the woodwork: floors, window and door frames, built-in cupboards. Several weeks' work. It would supplement the money he made on the furniture he created in our cellar. One consequence was he'd be better off for a while, another was that I had to take on more of the domestic jobs. He'd do the same if I got very busy. To date we'd never both been inundated at the same time.

I got Maddie and Tom from school and walked them back. I bunged potatoes in to bake, whizzed up coleslaw in the processor and grated cheese.

While the spuds cooked I sorted the clean clothes and put them in the kids' drawers, left Ray's pile on his bed, put mine away. I joined the children, who were watching a bizarre cartoon. I was completely baffled, unable to follow the plot or even tell what type of creatures the characters were meant to be.

'Why's she doing that?' I asked.

'Shush,' Maddie complained.

'She's saving him,' Tom explained.

'Shush.' Maddie rounded on Tom.

'Who's the blue one?' I said.

'Mummy,' Maddie said sharply, 'go away. You're ruining it.'

I went.

Agnes lived in a small red-brick terrace in Ladybarn. The house had colourful stained-glass panels at the sides of the front door. The woodwork was painted a deep jade green, an old-fashioned flavour. It was the sort of place that the estate agents describe as full of original features.

The creamy lace curtain moved when I drew up. Agnes looked out and waved. She was ready and waiting. Her white hair was carefully styled and she wore the same navy coat. I got out and opened the passenger door for her. She was nervous. She got the seat belt tangled up with her handbag and the more she struggled the worse it got.

'Here, let me sort that out.' I leant across and unwound everything, buckled the seat belt. Set off.

'Have you told Mrs Palmer we're coming?'

'Yes. I popped in on Tuesday after I'd been to see you. I don't know whether she took it in really. I said I'd be back later in the week, that I'd be bringing a friend. She didn't ask who.'

'We'd better agree on who I am, in case anyone asks. Perhaps we should pass me off as your niece or something like that.'

'No.' She was shocked. 'No, I'd rather a friend of the family.' Her hand worked away at the jet brooch on her coat. I'd obviously touched a nerve. A niece she preferred to forget? I couldn't ask about it. The colour had drained from her face and I needed to put her at ease before we reached Homelea.

'Fine,' I said. 'A friend of the family. Call me Sal – it sounds better than Miss Kilkenny. I prefer it anyway.'

'Yes, and you had better call me Agnes.'

'Are you sure?'

'Yes. I know a lot of my generation like to keep to the formalities but it really doesn't matter any more. There's hardly anyone left to call me Agnes now, you know.'

'OK. How was Mrs Palmer on Tuesday?'

'Very restless. Other times she just dozes off.'

'That could be the side effects of the medicine. Anyway, I just want to meet her today and get a look at the place. I've had a word with a GP I know and she's suggested we find out from Mrs Palmer's doctor exactly how the trouble started and what drugs she's on. It's possible that there's been a wrong diagnosis and that she hasn't got Alzheimer's at all. I was reading this book...'

'Acute confusional disorder,' said Agnes.

'Yes.' My surprise showed.

'I've been reading too,' she smiled. 'I got some books from the library.' She pointed. 'It's left here.'

We turned into a gravelled driveway between large stone gateposts. I parked in front of the house. It was a huge place with outbuildings beyond and a conservatory along one wall of the house. Homelea was probably

38

built by one of the Manchester merchants, a visible statement of his wealth and success. It even boasted a small turret on one corner.

I let Agnes lead the way. There was a ramp as well as steps up to the front porch. Agnes rang the bell. The door was opened promptly by a young woman who recognised her and invited us in. She disappeared. My first impression was of warmth and tasteful decoration, everything in cream, pale green and rose. The aroma of fresh coffee. The broad entrance hall had a large room off to each side, stairs ahead and more doorways at the bottom. Those led to the kitchen and dining room, I assumed. The door to our right was closed; I could hear the murmur of television. But Agnes went through to the room on our left.

This was a corner room with two bay windows. In the recess of the one at the front there was a table with high-backed chairs. A woman sat writing. In the other bay two women, deep in conversation, sat on a chintz-covered sofa. Each held a cat on her lap.

Around the rest of the large room were three clusters of high-backed easy chairs and side tables. People were sitting in some of these, reading papers and books, sewing and playing chess. The atmosphere was relaxed, quietly busy.

'She must be in the other room,' said Agnes.

We crossed the hall and opened the door. The room had the same decor but a semicircle of chairs faced us, arranged to focus on the television set, which was blaring out. There were six people there. A couple looked up as we went in. Agnes moved over to the woman sitting nearest to us, on the outside of the group.

'Lily, hello. How are you?'

The woman turned to face her. She stared blankly, unwavering, at Agnes for two or three seconds then turned back to the television set. I heard Agnes sigh. I put my hand on her arm. The poor woman. Her closest friend had no idea who she was.

CHAPTER FOUR

'Lily,' Agnes bent over close to her friend, 'it's me, Agnes. I've come to see you. Lily?'

'She had a bad night,' a man sitting in the centre of the semicircle spoke up, 'wandering about. They'll have given her something to calm her down.'

There was no response from Lily, who continued to stare at the television.

'I think there's too much of it myself,' the man continued, 'pills. Take a pill for anything these days. People go to see the doctor and they're not happy unless they come away with a bottle of tablets. Look at her, you couldn't say she was well, could you? Just keeping her quiet. Doped up.'

'Shush.' The woman on his left glared at him.

'I'm just saying they're too quick with their tablets. There's some folk in here would rattle if you shook 'em...'

'Be quiet, will you? I can't hear the television,' his neighbour admonished him.

A young woman wearing a maroon overall came into the room carrying a tray of drinks. Agnes asked her about Lily.

'You're best talking to Mrs Knight,' she suggested. 'I think she's in the office at the back. Do you know the way?'

Agnes nodded. She squeezed Lily's hand, told her she wouldn't be long and straightened up.

Mrs Knight, the matron, exuded competence and efficiency. She provided us with chairs, sent for cups of tea and made notes as we talked. She wore a dark blue nursing uniform and a hat. Her hair was thick and black and cut in a pageboy bob that seemed to emphasise her long face and drooping eyes.

Agnes introduced me as a family friend and asked about Lily.

'Mrs Palmer was rather disturbed in the night. I'm afraid she suffered some incontinence, which obviously distressed her, and she was quite hard to settle. She was given a sedative. That may have left her a little groggy.'

'She doesn't even recognise me,' said Agnes.

'I'm sorry,' said Mrs Knight. 'I realise how upsetting it must be for you. It is a common symptom but it won't necessarily persist. You may find a great improvement on your next visit.' The words were sympathetic but there was no warmth in her manner. 'Mrs Valley-Brown probably explained to you that we're dealing with a slow degenerative illness. It proceeds unevenly. Although we can't halt the disease we can make life as comfortable as possible for Mrs Palmer until such time as she needs additional care.'

'What would happen then?' I asked. Out of the corner of my eye I saw Agnes freeze, the teacup halfway to her mouth.

'Excellent care is provided at the psycho-geriatric unit at Kingsfield.'

Agnes' hand was shaking so badly that the cup clattered as she put it down. Everyone had heard of Kingsfield – one of the vast, old-style asylums.

'I thought it was shut,' I said. 'I thought they were closing all those places down.'

'Many wards did close and much of it has been put to other use but there's a very successful psycho-geriatric unit.' Mrs Knight seemed oblivious to Agnes' distress. 'The staff have a great deal of skill in dealing with confused and frail elderly people. We do recognise that community facilities aren't appropriate for some patients, or they simply aren't available. Kingsfield still has a role.'

Agnes cleared her throat. 'I was wondering whether Lily's problems might be due to a physical upset. There's something I've read about called acute confusional disorder.'

Mrs Knight nodded. 'The doctor ruled that out. The state you're referring to is quite easy to identify because we can connect the confusion to a particular physical illness. In Mrs Palmer's case there was no such link. She was given a complete medical on her arrival here. It's something we offer all our residents – we even arrange X-rays at the hospital so we can be absolutely sure that people have no physical problems that have gone undetected.'

'But it happened so swiftly,' Agnes went on, 'it wasn't gradual.'

'I know all the books talk about Alzheimer's progressing very slowly,' Mrs Knight clasped her hands on the table and leant forward as she spoke, 'but quite often early symptoms go unnoticed. Mrs Palmer may well have been forgetful for some time without it causing anyone undue concern. In a new environment some of these symptoms stand out more clearly.'

'She's always had an excellent memory,' insisted Agnes.

'That was just an example,' remarked Mrs Knight, unsmiling, 'but I've been in nursing for twenty-five years, I've specialised in geriatric care and I've no reason to think Mrs Palmer has acute confusional disorder rather than progressive dementia.' Subject closed.

'Who's her doctor?' I asked.

'Dr Goulden. He holds a regular surgery here every week. Mrs Palmer transferred when she moved in.'

'So we could ask him about this?' I ventured.

'By all means. But Dr Goulden is only

going to repeat what I've already told you.' Her voice was icy.

'Do you have his number?'

'Certainly.' She gave me it then rose from her chair. The interview was over. Then she made an effort to redeem the atmosphere. 'I hope he'll be able to set your minds at ease. We do feel it's important that friends and relatives have all the information they can about each individual care plan here.' Still no smile, though. It was unnerving. A missing bit of body language that made it feel that the whole conversation was askew. Well, the exchange had hardly been harmonious. Medical types sure don't like their judgement questioned.

Agnes wanted to sit with Lily for a while so we returned to the TV lounge. Lily didn't resist when Agnes sat beside her and took her hand. They were like that for ten minutes or more. Lily staring at the box, Agnes, her eyes cast down, looking up at her friend every now and then.

Lily was small, her feet barely reached the floor. Her neck craned forward and the top of her spine was curved with age. She had steel-grey hair, tightly permed. Her face was round, crosshatched with fine lines. A pair of modern glasses with pink and cream frames rested on her small nose. A trickle of saliva edged its way down from the side of her mouth. Agnes wiped it away with her hanky. Lily didn't notice.

I pretended to watch a feature on how to cook borscht.

Agnes stood up and said goodbye, told Lily she'd come again tomorrow, bent forward and kissed her cheek. No reaction.

We were halfway back to Agnes' house before she broke the silence. There were tears in her voice, and determination. 'I want you to see that doctor, talk to him about the diagnosis. I wasn't at all satisfied with that woman's explanation. She hardly gave much consideration to concerns.'

'Made up her mind already,' I said. 'People like that don't believe in uncertainties. She'd never admit they were wrong, I bet. Too much at stake. She was frosty, though, wasn't she? Did you notice she never smiled, not once?'

'It's all happened so quickly,' said Agnes, 'that's what I was trying to tell her. Lily got ill suddenly, not progressively, and today she's much worse.'

'You've never seen her like that before?' I asked.

'No. She's always known me, known...' she shook her head, grappling for words to explain, 'known herself, even if she's been quiet or distressed. I'm so worried.' She broke off.

I pulled up outside her house and turned the engine off. It ticked as the metal cooled.

'I want to see that doctor and I'd like you to be there. Sometimes people are a little dismissive because of my age. I realise you'll want a fee and I'll be happy to pay for your time. And I'll ring Charles, Lily's son. He should know. I'm sure he'd want to.'

'Is he close to his mother?'

'Not really. I think he functions on guilt. He sends money. He's a very busy man.' There was a bitter edge to her voice. 'I must sound harsh. It just seems so unfair. Still, I shall talk to him.'

'It might be worth contacting Lily's former GP as well,' I suggested. 'The doctor I talked to said to get the whole physical history, find out the order in which things happened.'

'Well, that's Dr Chattaway. He's my doctor, too. I'm sure he'll help if he can.'

'I'll try and make an appointment with Dr Goulden first,' I said. 'Are there any days that are bad for you, any regular appointments?'

'Nothing I can't break.' She smiled. 'So you don't think I'm being silly, wanting to

47

know more?'

'No, not in the least. In the end we might find that Goulden's diagnosis is right but there's enough doubt in my mind to ask a few more questions.'

Agnes nodded. 'Thank you. I'd never forgive myself if there was anything...' She sucked in a breath and let it go, unbuckled her seat belt. I got out and opened the door for her.

'I'll ring as soon as I've fixed a time.' I waited until she'd opened the front door before turning the ignition. She waved and I drove off. It was twelve thirty, I was ravenous and a Greek feast awaited.

CHAPTER FIVE

Rachel, my social worker contact, was one of life's great prattlers. She burbled on over stuffed vine leaves and tzatziki, vegetarian moussaka and kebabs. I'd never worked out whether she did this to her clients as well or whether behind closed doors a listener emerged – mouth shut and all ears.

We were sipping strong coffee from dinky

cups before she asked me about the case. I sketched it in for her without giving away anything that would break confidentiality.

'Check it out with the doctor,' she agreed. 'But there could well be a lot of denial going on, you know, from the friend. Alzheimer's is the new scare, worse than cancer. People are very frightened. It's understandable – you have to watch someone lose their identity, their personality. How do you keep loving someone who's not there any more?'

'She's no fool, the friend,' I defended Agnes.

'I'm not saying she is. You could always get a second opinion – ask her old GP to come and see her or get a referral to a consultant.' Rachel fished a sugar cube out of the bowl on her spoon.

I nodded. 'What about her social worker?'

'How do you mean?'

'I think there was a social worker involved with the move. Would they have made reports on the woman at the time, her state of mind and so on?'

'Oh, yes.' She lowered the spoon into the tiny cup, the sugar cube turned brown. 'There'd be case notes. Probably just the standard things, a general outline of the case, assessment of needs. But from what you've said the social worker might only have seen her once. She's not at risk. I wouldn't rely too much on finding anything very illuminating there.' She tipped the coffee-soaked cube into her mouth and sucked.

'Wouldn't they do any follow-up?'

'No need. The home's registered, they take responsibility for her care. Which one is it?'

I hesitated.

'It's all right,' Rachel laughed at my caution, 'I can keep a secret. It's just that there's a couple of places have got a bad name for themselves.'

'Homelea, on Wilbraham Road.'

She shook her head. 'Nope. Did it look OK?'

'Yeah.'

'Smell all right?'

'What?'

'It's a good indicator. If it stinks of piss or even boiled cabbage you know they're not doing all that they can.'

'No, it was fine, nice. People looked busy, you know. Well, apart from the TV lounge.'

Rachel laughed. 'There's always a TV lounge. Mind you, we've all got them, haven't we? Just looks different if you've a dozen people sat in high-backed chairs watching it.'

I asked Rachel a few more questions about

the role of Social Services in the care of older people. She told me that in the situation I'd described it would be peripheral. My research complete I sat back and listened while Rachel chuntered on and sucked sugar cubes.

I paid the bill wondering whether it hadn't been a rather pricey way of finding out virtually nothing. On the other hand I had enjoyed my time with Rachel. She was lively company, and when you work alone it's fun to have lunch out. Later, though I didn't know it then, her help was going to be invaluable. In a totally unexpected way.

There was a van parked outside the Dobsons', a white Transit with the words 'Swift Deliveries – Swinton' emblazoned in vivid red along the side and an arrow in flight underlining the message. A man sat in the front seat, reading a tabloid and smoking. He flicked his eyes from the paper to me as I turned to walk up the drive. A black guy with a serious haircut. A precisely honed wedge.

He wound down the window and called to me, 'Kilkenny's?'

'What is it?' I asked. I hadn't ordered anything, no deliveries due. Swift or otherwise.

'I rang you.' He cocked his head towards

the house. 'The answerphone.'

Aahh! Of course, the young man with no name. 'Yes. Come on in.'

He locked up the van and followed me up the path. In the office he agreed to coffee and introduced himself as Jimmy Achebe.

It was hard to judge his age, though he had a very young face, unlined coppery skin, black hair. Closer to I saw the sides and the back were shaved and the wedge section glistened with oil or gel. He wore gold rings in his ears and a gold wedding ring. He was drenched in eau de nicotine. I wondered whether he'd light up without asking. I don't keep an ashtray in the office. It's a deliberate policy to prevent people smoking there. You'd be amazed how many chronic smokers still try, offering desperately to 'use the bin/cup/saucer if you haven't an ashtray'. Jimmy Achebe wore a pale blue nylon zip-up boiler suit with the legend 'Swift Deliveries' embroidered on the back in red.

'So, how can I help? I gather you were interrupted yesterday.' I brought the mugs over to the desk.

'Yeah. Sorry 'bout that. My wife.' He took the coffee from me.

I sat down opposite him. Fished out a pad and pen.

He looked away, shrugged, fidgeted and sighed. 'Is it about your wife?'

He nodded, rubbed his nose with a broad palm. 'Yeah, I think there's something going on. She's out when she should be in. I'm not saying it's anything wrong, you know, but there's something going down.'

'Have you asked her about it?'

He sighed again. 'She gets all defensive, tells me I'm paranoid, that I'm going to ruin things between us. Says I have to trust her. She's been that moody, flies off the handle and that.' He frowned, at a loss how to deal with the situation.

'Tell me about her,' I suggested.

'What?' He glared as though the idea were somehow improper.

'What's she like? How did you meet her? When did you get married? What's her job?'

He groaned. 'She's called Tina. She's a fashion designer. She makes her own gear – jackets and that – tries to sell it on to the buyers. It's hard, though. She's tried for a few jobs in the trade but...' He shrugged. 'It gets her down sometimes. We've been married eighteen months. She's epileptic – that makes it harder to get the work. People think she's gonna have a fit every five minutes. I tell her not to say anything but she wants to be up-front about it. She's proud, you know, doesn't want to hide it but people just freak out.'

'Does she work from home?'

'Yeah. She tried renting some space in the craft village but that didn't last long. She says she needs some capital to get ahead. So now she uses the spare room.' He spread his hands.

'And you're a driver?'

'Yeah, money's crap but it's regular.' He glanced to see if his language had given offence. I smiled.

'OK. So tell me about recently. She's been going out a lot at night?'

'No, no. It's in the day. When I'm at work. A couple of times I've called home if I'm doing a delivery that way – grab a cuppa or some food – and she's not there. I asked her about it later, "What you done today?" and she said she'd just been in and when I said I'd been home she says, "Oh yeah, I went up the shops." I could tell she was lying. And the next time I asked her straight out, that's when she got all upset and that.'

'So this has happened twice?'

'More than that. Other times I've rung up. I hate checking up on her but I don't know what's going on. She won't talk to me about it. Your mind starts thinking all sorts, I mean all sorts. I know her regular things like aqua-fit and Fridays she likes to go down the market but this is different. She's keeping something from me.'

'Do you know how long she's out?'

He shrugged. 'A couple of hours.'

'Any particular days?'

'Middle of the week, I think.'

I thought about the way he'd described her moods. 'She ever use drugs?'

He grinned and shook his head. 'Only for the illness.'

'What do you want me to do?' I asked him.

'Find out,' he said. 'Find out where she's going, what she's doing. Watch her, follow her, whatever you have to do.' He waved his arm as he spoke, pushing the problem my way. 'Shit, I hate this,' he said.

'OK. Let me suggest something. First of all try and talk to Tina about it again. Tell her, you're worried, that you don't want secrets in the marriage, ask her straight out to tell you what's going on. Now if she won't or if you're not happy with what she does tell you then you can come back to me. I charge a hundred pounds a day for surveillance, minimum. I might have to watch the house for several days.'

He took a sharp breath in.

'Think about it,' I said. 'It's worth bearing in mind you may be paying for bad news. Tina's keeping something from you, so there's a danger it'll be something you'll find very difficult. I may find she's having an affair – it could be something like that – but even if it's completely innocent the fact of you using an investigator to spy on her could break up your marriage anyway.'

'Don't you think I haven't thought about all that?' he protested. 'But knowing – at least I'd know.' He rubbed his nose again. 'If she was cheating on me I'd know where I stood. If it was something else,' he shrugged, 'maybe I'd not even tell her but I'd know. Now, it's like I'm drowning.' He frowned and looked away. I saw his Adam's apple bob up and down.

'OK,' I said. 'Think it over, try and talk to Tina again, then take it from there.'

'Right, thanks.'

We stood up. At the door Jimmy turned. 'About the money – can I pay it in instalments, if it's a fair bit? You don't need it all at once?'

'No problem. By the way, if you do want me to do the work I'll need a photo of Tina.'

'Yeah, right.'

He'd lit the fag before he hit the pavement.

I wrote up my notes so they'd make sense another day. Then I rang the number for Dr Goulden. An answer-phone told me the surgery was closed, would open again at four o'clock and then gave me an emergency number to ring. That seemed a bit drastic so I hung fire.

There was a heavy metallic sky and an unnerving pressure that made my eyeballs ache. The storm broke just as the kids emerged from school. Resounding cracks of thunder and great belching rumbles had half the playground in hysterics. The raindrops were the extra-large variety that bounced as they hit the pavement. It kept it up for half an hour but even then didn't have the decency to move on and dry up. Instead drizzle settled in. I closed the curtains and lit the lamps.

I got through to Dr Goulden's receptionist who arranged an appointment for the Monday afternoon. I explained we weren't patients but needed to see the doctor about a member of the family at Homelea. (Not strictly true but I didn't want to fail at the blood-relatives hurdle.) As it was, the computer couldn't cope with information outside of its programme, it needed a patient, so in the end the appointment was made in Lily Palmer's name.

Dr Chattaway, Agnes' GP and formerly Lily's, didn't have an appointment system. It was turn up and wait. I asked the receptionist when the quietest surgery was.

'Oh, it's always busy,' she said, 'but Monday's by far the worst.'

When I rang Agnes she suggested we try Tuesday morning. 'We'd still have fresh in our minds what Dr Goulden said ... and I wouldn't want to leave it any longer than necessary. So, Tuesday, I think.'

'Fine,' I said. 'When I see you on Monday we'll fix up a time for the Tuesday morning. And once we've seen both doctors we can assess where we're up to.'

'Whether it's all a waste of time.'

'No, I didn't mean...'

'I'm sorry,' she said, 'it's difficult to remain even-tempered sometimes. I do appreciate your help.'

There wasn't anything to do on the case until Monday. It was Thursday night. A three-day weekend then, one of the perks of part-time hours. And if I got some of the chores out of the way while the children were at school on the Friday there'd be more time for enjoying ourselves at the weekend proper. We'd go down to the park and gardens at Fletcher Moss. It often flooded in the winter, but with wellies on, floods could be fun. I'd take Maddie and Tom swimming too or maybe to the pictures. My budget wouldn't stretch to visits to the big plush cinemas but I could manage an occasional treat at the local picture house. I'd have to ring Cine City, find out what was on. Plenty to do, and more than enough to occupy my mind and stop me puzzling over Lily Palmer's condition.

CHAPTER SIX

First thing Monday morning Jimmy Achebe rang. I hadn't even opened the post. He spoke hurriedly. He wanted me to do the job, he'd drop off a photo later that day. I reminded him to include his address, his home phone number and a note of any regular appointments Tina had. There was no point in my trailing her to aqua-fit and back, then billing him for it. Were there any days in particular he wanted me to cover?

'Maybe tomorrow and Wednesday – it's

usually mid-week.'

'And you tried asking Tina about it?'

'Yeah. She wasn't having any of it. Told me I was imagining things, says she's not hiding anything. Told me to stop harassing her.' I heard him blow out in exasperation. 'Look, about the money. I'll get what I can today but the rest, well, like I said...'

'Don't worry, I'll check back with you each time I've done a stint. That way, if it starts mounting up you can ask me to stop. How can I get in touch?'

'I'll have to ring you,' he said, 'but you can leave a message here at work. You've got the number, haven't you?'

'Yeah.'

'Just say you want me to ring. They'll pass it on. I hate this. I feel like I'm the one doing something wrong.'

'Do you want to think it over a bit longer?'

'No. It's cracking me up. I just want it sorted.'

There was a lull in my morning after I'd opened and binned the post. I went swimming. Thirty lengths of the local pool and a reasonably hot shower. I emerged into the blank February weather feeling loose-limbed and smug.

Back home Ray had left a note on the

kitchen table: 'Harry knows someone looking for room. Sheila. May ring.'

My heart dipped. In order to make ends meet we needed to let out the attic flat. We rented the house from an ex-lecturer of mine. He'd gone out to do a year in Australia and they kept renewing his contract. We had to cover the mortgage, bills and maintain the place.

Our first lodgers, Joanne and Christine, had been great but they'd moved on once they'd saved enough for a deposit on a place of their own. Their successor, Clive, was the lodger from hell. Since we'd got him out we'd taken a succession of short-term lets: an actor appearing at the Royal Exchange, a teacher who needed a bolt-hole while her damp-proof course was done and a German sociologist who was doing a term at the university. They were all a vast improvement on Clive but each time there was the disruption of getting used to a new face at the breakfast table, of negotiating use of the kitchen, the bath and the fridge. And in between we were short on income. We really needed a permanent person but I was still terrified we might end up with another complete wally. My old friend Harry wouldn't deliberately send me a plonker but sometimes they could be hard to spot.

Not long after lunch I collected Agnes and we drove over to Dr Goulden's surgery. It was part of a large detached house. Brass plaques on the gatepost and front door showed it also housed Jason and Evers, Architects, and Mowbray Insurance Services. The front gardens had been tarmacked over for parking. Dr Goulden used the downstairs rooms. Reception and waiting room to the left, consulting room to the right.

The receptionist clicked us off on the computer and directed us to the waiting room. Three women were already there. No one spoke to anyone else or made eye contact.

Agnes leant over to whisper to me. 'When we go in,' she said, 'I'll explain what we want.'

I agreed. 'You do the talking.'

We were another tedious twenty minutes waiting. I leafed through Marie Claire and Vogue. Gradually each of the three women was summoned by the buzzer and the illuminated sign inviting 'Next patient please', and disappeared. Then it was our turn.

Dr Goulden welcomed us with a bright smile.

'Mrs Palmer.' He shook Agnes by the hand and gestured to the seat at the side of his desk.

'I'm Miss Donlan,' said Agnes. 'We've come about–'

'I'm sorry,' he interrupted, the smile replaced by a puzzled look, 'but I seem to have the wrong notes here.'

'No, they're right,' said Agnes, sitting down. 'We've come about Mrs Palmer.'

'Aah.' He regained his composure and fetched an extra chair over from the far corner of the room for me.

'So,' he held his hands open to Agnes, 'how can I help?'

While she explained the situation and her worries I studied Dr Goulden. He was probably in his early thirties, with a square face, thick blond hair, pale blue eyes, sandy freckles. Tall, big-boned. He was impeccably dressed in blue striped shirt, dark blue suit and tie. He probably had to shop at Long and Tall or whatever that specialist shop is called. He sounded solid middle class, no trace of a regional accent. He listened attentively, his head cocked to one side just so you'd know he was listening attentively.

When Agnes had finished he said, 'I'd just like to clarify a few points. You are a friend of Mrs Palmer's and this is...' He looked at me.

'A friend of the family,' said Agnes, 'Sal, Sally.'

63

I winced visibly. People have a habit of softening my name. But I've never been a Sally. Sal was a pet name my dad used. My real name's Sarah but I've been Sal as long as I can remember. Sally makes me feel like a six-year-old.

'Mmm,' Dr Goulden didn't sound all that keen, 'Mrs Palmer's son is actually listed as next of kin.'

'But he's in Exeter,' said Agnes. 'I talked to him on Friday, he'd no objection to me making the appointment. He knows I visit Lily two or three times a week.' Agnes began to sound defensive.

'I don't discuss my patients with other people. Confidentiality is paramount. I'm sure you understand. Mrs Palmer is getting the very best care, Homelea has an excellent reputation—'

'We could go to the trouble of arranging for Mr Palmer to travel up from Devon to put these questions to you,' I said, 'but it seems rather an extreme measure, a waste of time for everyone concerned. We've already spoken to Mrs Knight and I'm not aware that there has been any problem about patient confidentiality. If you could answer some of Miss Donlan's queries we wouldn't need to trouble you any further.'

There was an uncomfortable pause. We sat it out.

He decided to play ball. 'Your concern is that Mrs Palmer may be suffering from an acute confusion rather than chronic decline?'

Agnes nodded.

Dr Goulden smiled sympathetically. 'I'm ninety-nine per cent certain that's not the case but if you'll bear with me I'll scan the notes and see if we could have missed anything.' He leafed through the papers humming tunelessly. 'Tum-ti-tum-ti-tum-tum-tum', a gesture intended to show us that all was well, to demonstrate how competent and relaxed he was.

He patted the papers back into the manila folder. 'No,' he said, 'nothing. I'd have been very surprised if there had been. In the sort of case you're asking about,' he explained, 'we'd look for a certain sort of physical problem, an untreated infection, perhaps, from which we could date the development of the confusion. Now we've nothing like that here, absolutely nothing.' He stressed the words. 'She had a full medical on arrival at Homelea, sort of MOT,' he smiled insincerely and waved the folder, 'and everything I've seen of Mrs Palmer makes me certain that she has chronic dementia, Alzheimer's. I'm sorry. I can assure you we are doing our best for her.'

Agnes suddenly looked much older, the brilliance of her dark eyes dulled. 'But it's all been so quick,' she said. 'She doesn't know who I am any more.'The last words came out in a whisper as she fought to stay in control.

'There are peaks and troughs,' said Dr Goulden, 'as with any chronic disease. The situation may well improve. Often adjusting the medication can help things considerably. With some patients the situation can stabilise and remain so for many months.'

'What medicine is she getting?' I asked.

He looked at me. That smile again. 'She's currently receiving a controlled-dose tranquilliser, what we call an antipsychotic drug, and she's given something to help her sleep if Mrs Knight judges it to be necessary. Drugs have a very useful role in Mrs Palmer's therapy but we use them with caution. The tranquilliser, for example, wouldn't be given on a long-term basis.'

'Is it one of the phenothiazines?' I asked, remembering what I'd read in Moira's books and hoping I'd got the pronunciation right. 'What dosage is she on?'

This time the smile was accompanied by a patronising tilt of the head. 'I don't see that such detail is of much help to the layperson in understanding our care plan.'

'We'd like to know,' I said. No explanation, no justification.

He cleared his throat and rustled papers. 'Thioridazine,' he said. 'Twenty-five milligrams twice daily. And nitrazepam for the insomnia as required.'

'There can sometimes be side effects, can't there?' asked Agnes. 'The drugs themselves can cause confusion in some people, make things worse.'

'Yes, on occasion. All drugs carry some risk of minor side effects. But on the whole we feel the benefits far outweigh any risks. I can assure you I'll be monitoring the response to the medication very carefully. There's usually a settling-down period before the situation stabilises. If I see any indication of an adverse reaction I'll reduce or withdraw the medication. I'd be hoping to gradually phase it out anyway. As I say, it's not something I see Mrs Palmer requiring on a long-term basis.'

'And you don't think any of her symptoms are due to the drugs themselves?' I asked.

'No, definitely not. The confusion and agitation were what indicated the need for treatment in the first place. They've not arisen as a reaction to the medicines, they were present before the drug therapy started.' He placed Lily's notes on top of the neat stack on his desk. 'Once the situation has stabilised, as I'm sure it will, I think we'll see substantial improvement and we'll have a much calmer and more relaxed patient.'

He stood up and picked up Lily's notes, batting them gently against his other hand as he waited for us to leave. Agnes went ahead of me. As she opened the door I glanced back into the room. Dr Goulden was standing at his filing cabinet putting the notes away. But it was his reflection in the mirror above the cabinet that caught my attention. His face was contorted with rage, lips drawn back, taut and white, teeth bared, eyes glaring. My stomach lurched. It was an astonishing sight. I slipped out before he noticed me looking.

It was curiosity made me return to the building. I found it hard to credit what I'd seen and wanted to nose around a bit more. I settled Agnes in the car and then claimed to have left my gloves in the waiting room. The lobby was deserted – we must have been the last appointment.

The words from the consulting room were a little muffled behind the closed door, but I could make out most of what Goulden said, particularly at such a loud volume. 'I do not see friends and relatives. I'm a doctor, not a bloody support group. I see patients. You make appointments for patients.' He was furious, spitting out the words, ladling on scorn and derision. 'Next time you decide to offer appointments to Uncle Tom Cobley and all just use your bloody brains, woman.'

I heard a murmur in reply.

'Tell them you only make appointments for registered patients. Show some initiative, for Christ's sake. Anything else, you check with me first. Got it?'

Another murmur.

'I've enough to do without being at the beck and call of every silly old bat who gets a bee in her bonnet. They read an article in some half-cocked magazine and next minute they're God's gift to medicine. Check next time and if they're not patients...'

I left. I'd heard enough and I didn't want the receptionist to know I'd witnessed her humiliation.

In the car Agnes was deflated. Goulden's certainty about Lily's illness had put paid to any hope she might have had about mis-diagnosis. And he had given us the inform-ation we asked for even though we'd had to lean on him to get it. But she hadn't seen what I had, nor heard him just now.

'I think he's hiding something,' I said. 'He

hated having to see us, he didn't want to talk to us about Lily.'

I described to Agnes the expression I'd seen on Goulden's face as I was leaving and the way he'd bawled out his receptionist.

'He was – beside himself,' I said. 'That makes me wonder, why did our visit upset him to such a degree?'

'Perhaps he's just a very angry man. Choleric they used to call it.'

'I don't like him,' I said, 'and I wouldn't trust him as far as I can spit.'

CHAPTER SEVEN

Dr Chattaway used an end terraced house for his surgery. Plastic chairs were arranged around the walls of the room. On a table in the centre were copies of People's Friend, National Geographic and Woman's Own. The waiting room was full. No intercom here. The doctor stuck his head round the door every few minutes and asked for the next patient. People shuffled along each time.

Gradually we moved around the room and finally we reached the inner sanctum. Dr

Chattaway motioned to chairs and settled behind his highly polished desk. It was huge; they probably had to dismantle it to get it through the doorway. On the wall were framed diplomas and a photograph of Dr Chattaway in cap and gown.

'Miss Donlan,' he grinned, 'how are you? I haven't seen you for a while.' His accent blended Indian consonants and Mancunian vowels.

Agnes explained why we'd come. He listened politely, rolling a thick fountain pen between his fingers and frowning slightly. When she'd finished he nodded once.

'Of course I no longer have Mrs Palmer's notes. As you know, I treated Mrs Palmer for the fall, the shoulder, and that was mending fine, but she was keen to move into sheltered accommodation. I didn't see her again, she transferred to Dr Goulden. I'm sorry to hear she's so poorly.'

I asked him if Lily had ever shown any signs of dementia.

She hadn't. But neither had she had any acute illness that could have led to dementia-like symptoms. He recommended that we ask Dr Goulden to make sure there was no adverse reaction to drugs she was prescribed. 'It's a common enough problem,' he said. 'All

71

drugs have side effects and sometimes switching to another similar drug can bring great improvements. I must say I am surprised that she is so ill. I would agree it seems very sudden and if she were my patient I would be reviewing the drugs very carefully.'

As Dr Goulden claimed he was.

There was nothing else he could tell us. I drove Agnes home and she invited me in.

We sat in the front room, peaceful and homely. It still had the original fireplace with its ceramic tiles showing dog roses and rosehips, and a picture rail ran round the room. Agnes had decorated in warm colours, gold and peach and a spicy brown. She lit the coal-effect gas fire and we pulled our chairs up close. From somewhere else in the house a clock chimed, a sound from the days before time was measured in bleeps and digital displays.

'Is that it, then?' She looked into the fire.

'You can always get a second opinion – about Lily's condition now. I think you should consider that. Or a transfer. See about her changing back to Dr Chattaway, perhaps? Talk to Charles about it, he might need to make the request.'

She nodded then turned to look at me. 'And you. What do you think?'

'I'm not a doctor,' I objected.

'But you have an opinion?' Her dark eyes glittered.

'I don't know. I don't like Dr Goulden but that doesn't mean he doesn't know his job. I can't make a medical judgement, and the whole thing seems to hinge on that. Maybe it just happened more quickly for Lily, maybe the drugs do need looking at again like Dr Chattaway suggested. Either way there's not much I can usefully do at the moment. You need more medical help, not a private investigator.'

Agnes turned away, looked back at the flames. 'I can't believe I was wrong,' she murmured. 'Stubborn. How much do I owe you?'

'I can send you a bill.'

'I'd rather settle it now.'

'There's only really the doctors' visits, a bit of research. Fifty pounds will cover it.'

She left the room. Came back with the cash. I took the bills and folded them into my bag. 'Thank you.' I wanted to apologise but I didn't know what for.

On the doorstep she laid her hand on my arm. 'Thank you. For listening. It didn't turn out as I hoped but it helped to have someone taking it seriously.'

'Take care,' I said. 'If anything else crops

up you know where I am.'

As I walked away disappointment tightened my throat. If only it could've turned out differently. I thought it was all over then.

And we all know what thought did.

It was only ten forty-five and Tuesday was one of the days that Jimmy Achebe had asked me to watch Tina. I drove back to the office, checked my answerphone and mail and collected the camera. I'd invested in a powerful zoom lens which meant I could get shots of people without being under their noses. Nevertheless I still felt completely exposed whenever I used it. It was beyond me how anyone could fail to spot the strange woman parked in the car snapping away with a funny-looking camera. But to date no one had come up and knocked on the window to ask me my business. The zoom meant I could furnish my clients with the proof they wanted of lies told and trust betrayed.

Before leaving I rang Jimmy Achebe's home number. No point in staking out an empty house. Tina answered the phone.

'Hello,' I said, 'is that the travel agent's?'

'You've got the wrong number.'

'Oh, sorry.'

I stopped to buy a trendy sandwich and a

drink on the way across to the Achebes'. Levenshulme – where the biscuit factory sweetens the air. I drove past the address Jimmy had given me. An ordinary terrace. Door leading straight on to the street. A quiet road. One where a strange car parked too long would have the nets twitching. I parked up on the main road where I could see down the length of their street if Tina appeared.

I'd finished my posh butties (avocado, cream cheese and chives) and my drink. I was parked near the Antique Hypermarket, full of stalls dealing in furniture, fixtures and fittings. The sort of place you could get original fireplaces like Agnes' among the Victorian hatstands and chaises longues. I'd tagged along when my friend Diana had got old chimney pots there for her back yard. I divided my attention between Tina's street and the comings and goings of the antique dealers.

It was one thirty when she came out. The photo I had was a good likeness. She was short and slight. She walked down to the main road and turned left towards the shops. Once she'd passed the bus stop I slipped my camera in my bag, left the car and followed her at a safe distance.

Tina bought fresh milk and bread, a

chicken, vegetables. She called in the hardware shop and browsed and did the same in a cheap and cheerful clothes shop. Then she walked back home.

Some you win, some you lose.

CHAPTER EIGHT

Sheila was on the phone, the woman about the room. I told her what we'd got available and what it cost, a bit about the setup (two adults – not involved with each other – each with a child, one dog, shared kitchen and bathroom, no smoking). She was still interested but would be away for a few days on a field trip. I told her I'd check when Ray was in and fix a time for her to come and meet us. I took her number.

I rang Swift Deliveries and left a message for Jimmy Achebe to ring Kilkenny's after ten the following morning.

Moira's books were still in their carrier bag in the corner so I stuck them in the car ready to drop off the next time I passed her house or the surgery.

Over tea I got some times from Ray when

we could both be in to see Sheila. I rang her back while he was washing up and fixed for her to call Wednesday next week after tea. We wanted her to meet the kids but not until they'd been fed. Maddie in particular was capable of horrendous behaviour. I thought of it as attention-seeking in my better moments, and I didn't want to give her a chance to display it with food at hand.

That evening it was my turn to get the children to bed, a long process that included baths and books and stories. I also had to arbitrate in the many disputes that arose between the pair of them. Maddie and Tom were virtual opposites in looks as well as temperament. Tom had inherited Ray's dark curls, brown eyes and olive skin, while Maddie was dirty blonde, blue-eyed and pallid. Tom had a cheerful lust for life and experience; a sensuality that led him to wallow in mud and chuck himself all over the place. Maddie found the world an un-nerving place, was cautious, suspicious of the new, and a borderline hypochondriac. She could be infuriating but I loved her with a passion that continued to startle me.

Once I'd got them in pyjamas and per-suaded them to their beds, I had to check under beds, in drawers and behind curtains for scary things. Maddie was in an anxious phase and every shadow and sound had her gasping. When I'd done my atheistic version of casting out the devils and blessing the bedroom I sat in the old rocking chair in the corner of the room and began a story. They were both still awake when I finished.

'Will you stay, Mummy?' Maddie asked.

'Yes,' I sighed.

'Till I'm asleep?'

'Yes. Now be quiet.'

I closed my eyes and let my mind flow around the day's work. Images floated into my thoughts and away: Agnes' fireplace, Tina shopping, Dr Chattaway rolling his pen...

I jerked awake, a sour taste in my mouth. I could hear steady breathing from Maddie. I got up and bent over Tom, no sound at all. I touched his chin, he shuffled and sighed. I let my breath out and left them to it.

In the lounge with a fresh cup of tea I dug out my gardening books and spent an hour gazing at glossy pictures and looking up various species. In the depths of February it was hard to recall the scents and colours of the summer, to remember exactly how it felt when the sun went down four hours later and washing dried on the line. Of course, living in Manchester summer could often feel like February but we did have glimpses of the seasonal changes the rest of the country took as read.

I could hear Ray messing about in the cellar, fitting in a bit of his furniture making. When he'd a building job on everything else got postponed, so if he'd said yes to a few orders he'd soon have impatient customers ringing up wanting to know when the chest, table or chair would be finished.

He popped his face round the door to tell me he was taking Digger out for his walk. I was in bed and fast asleep before they came back.

After leaving the children at school I spent most of the money that Agnes had given me on food. I raced round the discount supermarket plucking cereal boxes and containers of milk and juice, toilet rolls, tins of beans and tomatoes, mini yoghurts, crisps, rice, cheap cheese, tea and coffee. In the vegetable shop opposite I picked a selection of vegetables and a bag full of fruit. I unloaded the lot on the kitchen table, stuck the cheese, yoghurts and milk in the fridge. The rest I'd sort out later. It was time for work.

Jimmy rang as requested just as I'd settled at my desk. 'I'm ringing from work,' he said.

'We're not meant to make private calls. I can't talk for long.'

In the background I could hear the sound of vans and a Tannoy.

'I watched Tina yesterday,' I said. 'And she didn't go anywhere but the local shops. Do you want me to try again today?'

'Yeah.'

'OK. Ring me again tomorrow, same time.'

I didn't want to alert Tina by using the old wrong number call again, so I just drove over to Levenshulme as soon as I could. After an hour sitting in the car my left buttock had seized up. I was getting hungry too. I'd demolished my apple and banana in the first half-hour. My stomach was growling. A light rain finally made it down from the clutches of the clouds. Fine as a sea fret and bringing with it the scent of sewage, not brine.

Tina came out wearing a check jacket, black skirt and carrying a bag. She looked stylish. Her hair was bound up in a knot on her head and she wore large gold earrings.

I got out of the car and locked it while she walked down the main road. She passed the bus stop and turned left towards the post office and the local train station. I followed her up the ramp and stood behind her while she bought a return to Piccadilly; I did too.

She took a seat in the waiting room while I went and stood on the platform. I didn't want to become too familiar.

When the train arrived I sat in a different coach. I looked out over East Manchester, Beswick, Ardwick, Miles Platting. I could spot the curve of the Velodrome changing the skyline and work going on to complete the large-scale redevelopment of the whole area. Where once there'd been whole estates of terraced houses, established communities, there were now great tracts of raw earth littered with heaps of bricks and huge concrete cylinders. Yellow cranes and earth movers gnawed away at the land.

Where had all the people gone? Would they come back or were homes going to be replaced by industrial estates, superstore complexes and yet more roads?

We were at Piccadilly in ten minutes. The check jacket made it easy to keep Tina in view. She took the escalator down to the Metrolink. Were we just going shopping or would I need a ticket to Bury or Altrincham? Tina didn't bother with a ticket. I hedged my bets and pressed the buttons to get a ticket for the central zone. Last thing I wanted was to get done for fare dodging.

The first tram was for Bury and she

boarded it. But we only went as far as Piccadilly Gardens. We weren't going shopping, though. She turned in the other direction and I followed her, at a distance, across Portland Street and along a side road to the Worcester Hotel. I waited while she went in, counted to twenty and then as quietly as I could opened the heavy glass door and followed. I was dead lucky, the receptionist wasn't at her desk. The place looked decent enough, good maroon wool carpet, clean decor, fresh lilies at reception, which made the lobby smell sweet. There was no lift. I took the stairs two at a time and as silently as possible, alert to any noises. The corridor on the first floor was empty. I thought I caught a footfall from upstairs. On the second landing I was in time to see a glimpse of Tina's check jacket disappearing into a room. Bingo!

I walked down to the room, number 203. I paused outside, stilling my breath and straining to catch any sound. Nothing. Just my pulse pounding, that sweet way it does when I'm scared of being caught.

There was nowhere in the corridor to wait. There were three doors on either side and a fire door at the far end. More than likely that would lead out to a fire escape. No good waiting out there, I wanted to see if anyone came up to join Tina.

I went back down to the first floor, prepared to act as if I were just leaving my room if anyone spotted me. Ten minutes crawled by. Then I heard footsteps, the clink of coins or keys. A man crossed the landing and carried on up. I followed him. He knocked sharply on a door and cast a glance my way as I appeared from the stairs. Room 203. The door opened and he went in. Full house.

I went down to the lobby. The receptionist was back, and she seemed surprised to see me.

'Can I help you?' she said.

I weighed her up. Young, lots of make-up, expensive clothes. It couldn't be very exciting working here. Maybe I could brighten her day. 'You might be able to,' I said. 'I'm a private detective.' I pulled out one of my cards and showed her. She took it, read it, handed it back. Cool. Sceptical. Weighing me up too.

'Room 203,' I said, 'can you tell me who's registered there?'

'I don't think I could do that,' she said, a neutral tone. 'Confidentiality and all that.'

'I thought that was doctors and priests,' I said.

'And lawyers,' she was enjoying this, 'and banks.' I missed the hint.

'You could just check the mail,' I gestured towards the pigeonholes, 'or tidy the information board. And I could just glance at the visitors' book.'

She sighed. 'Rotten wages,' she said, 'hotel and catering trade. Time they agreed a minimum wage.'

It took me a moment to cotton on. I nodded. Took a fiver from my purse, put it on the desk.

She smiled. 'Then there's inflation, the recession, negative equity. You know my house is worth less now than it was in 1989.' I placed a second fiver on the desk. 'Just look at those letters, what a mess.'

She turned away, pocketing the fivers, and began to shuffle the envelopes. I swivelled the ledger round my way. I found room 203, in the name of Mrs Peters. A flick back through the pages revealed another eight occasions. Mrs Peters checked in for days not nights. I made a note of the dates.

'Does Mr Peters always join her?' I asked.

The receptionist put the letters back and turned round.

Before she could answer, the door opened and a woman swept in carrying an umbrella and pulling a scarf from her neck.

'Sorry I'm late, Lynn.' She lifted the

counter top up and joined her colleague. 'Flipping plumbers. Plonkers more like.'

'I'm sorry we can't help you,' said Lynn very firmly. 'We don't use outside caterers.' End of conversation.

I'd done my job, bar the photos. I hadn't promised Jimmy Achebe photographic proof of what I discovered but it always helped to have hard evidence to back up the facts.

I loitered near the hotel for another hour watching people come and go and feeling faint from hunger before the man I'd seen emerged. He was in his forties, I guessed. Tall and slim. He wore an expensive camel coat and his brown hair was swept back from his face. He had a creamy complexion, clean-shaven. I got a shot of him in profile and another, full length, facing me. I swung the camera around and clicked the skyline just in case.

I soaked up nearly another hour of steady drizzle. My bladder began to ache, and my shoulder, too, a gnawing pain, a reaction to the tension. Tina came out. I snapped her twice then put my camera away. I stuck with her until she reached the platform at Piccadilly from where the train for Levenshulme left, then I called it a day. I had a blissful pee in the ladies' at the station, bought a huge sandwich, a rich chocolate bun and a large fresh coffee. Only when I'd eaten my fill and warmed through did I get the train myself. It was an old model, shabby and seedy. People were returning from work. I sat crushed in with the smell of wet wool and hair, and the windows grey with condensation. The train lurched to Levenshulme. I walked back and got my car. I didn't relish telling Jimmy what I'd found out. If Tina's meeting had been with a man at a café, a pub or a restaurant there may well have been an innocent explanation. But a hotel? A private room with a bed?

My job was done. Their troubles were just beginning.

CHAPTER NINE

I'd arranged for the kids to go home with school friends. On the way to get them I dropped the film in at a photo shop I know where they boast processing within the hour. I didn't need it that urgently. I'd collect it in the morning.

I reached the children at five.

'I could've given them tea, you know,' said Jean.

'We want tea, stay for tea,' Maddie began to chant and the others joined in.

'No, not tonight. Maybe some other time,' I said. I thanked Jean for offering, wishing she'd not mentioned it in front of the children. Now I was the mean, horrible Mummy who wouldn't let them.

After ten minutes of gathering up paintings, coats, lunch boxes and shoes I managed to remove Maddie and Tom, ignoring the protests and complaints.

It only took fifteen minutes to get tea on the table: three-minute macaroni and cheese sauce, tomato salad and bread and butter. Once fed the children crawled off to play puppies with Digger. The dog treated the whole thing with detached caution, poised to remove himself if any indignities were committed.

Ray got back from work and went for a shower. I warmed through his pasta and washed up the rest of the dishes. 'Your mother would have a fit,' I said.

'What do you mean?' he asked.

'It's three-minute macaroni,' I said.

'What? You haven't made fresh?'

'Nope.'

'Neither does she,' he said. 'Well, only to impress. She's got a cupboard full of tinned spaghetti hoops, you know.'

'She hasn't!'

'Yeah. She's not stupid,' he said. 'She might not admit it but she's discovered there's more to life than home cooking.'

'Like the bookies.'

'Definitely the bookies.'

Nana Tello – her real name is Costello but Tom's baby version had stuck – had a penchant for the horses. Ray spent a lot of time worrying about whether she was getting into debt or betting within her means. She refused point-blank to discuss it with him and denied it a lot of the time, like addicts do.

I liked her gambling. It proved she had weaknesses like the rest of us. Whenever she started on about how a good cook or a good mother or a good homemaker should do things I could conjure up an image of her entering her bets in a smoke-filled office.

As far as she was concerned our silly setup was a diversion from Ray's (Raymundo, as she called him) real need to find a pretty young mother for his poor motherless child. She couldn't accept that our arrangement was platonic and equitable. She veered between casting me as a hussy, a landlady or a

housekeeper. Ours wasn't an easy relationship.

Once the children were settled I claimed
the sofa. I flicked the channels hoping
against hope that they'd got the listings
wrong in the paper: football, darts, a TV
movie (all big hair and heroism in the face of
fatal illness) and a documentary. I watched
this latter for a few minutes. They were uncovering abuse in private old people's
homes. Everything from verbal cruelty and
petty bullying to systematic physical and
sexual abuse. I kept seeing Agnes and Lily in
place of the brave faces on the screen. I
recalled the savagery of Dr Goulden's face in
the mirror. He'd been livid at our enquiries.
Again I wondered why he'd reacted so
strongly.

I zapped the TV. What would Agnes do
now? She'd been so certain that something
was awry and we'd found nothing. She had
to face the inevitability of her friend's illness
and eventual death, though she could go on
for years. In the books I'd read there were
examples of people who had lost all sense of
who they were, who no longer recognised
family or friends, who'd lost all personality
and needed constant care and reassurance.
It would be hard for Lily but it'd probably

be harder for Agnes to watch her friend disappear.

It was too depressing. I sought out my library book. A bit of Patricia Cornwell, forensic sleuthing, stateside – just the ticket.

I made sure I was in my office in plenty of time the next morning for Jimmy Achebe's call. He rang a little after ten. I'd already decided to ask him to come in and see me; I didn't want to go into details over the phone.

'Hello, Jimmy. I've got some information for you. I ought to say it doesn't look very good.'

'Oh, right.' He sounded uncertain, very young.

'Perhaps if you called over after work?'

'Erm, yeah right.' I could only just hear him above the noise of the depot.

'What time do you finish?' I asked.

''Bout five. I'll be there just after.'

'OK. I'll see you then.'

The guy would be in purgatory all day.

I rang Ray at the site to see if he could get back before five. No problem. Relief. I wouldn't have to ring round sorting out a babysitter for a half-hour meeting.

I called at the photo shop and picked up the prints. They weren't brilliant but they'd do.

Back at my desk I pulled out the file I'd opened and wrote up my notes on the investigation. I always listed in detail the job I'd done. Just in case. Then I added up the time I'd spent following Tina; and my expenses. The tenner to the receptionist, the rail and Metro fares, even the food I'd bought at the station.

I'd learned the hard way that it all adds up. It's tough enough to make a living without being soft about the real costs of a case. I prepared the bill for Jimmy Achebe.

Later that morning I got an enquiry from someone wanting a night watchman. I passed them on to a firm I know in Stockport. After that it was very quiet. I tidied files and finally admitted to myself I was time-wasting.

I walked back home, pleased to see the pale sun had succeeded in emerging from the clouds. There were even a few wisps of blue sky. The ground was damp but not frozen. I'd be able to do some pottering in the garden.

For a couple of hours I lost myself in the pungent odour of damp earth and vegetation, the feel of brick and mud and dead wood, as I repaired the low wall of the herb garden, tidied up shrubs and prepared a sweet pea trench.

The children were tired on the way back

from school and dived for the telly when we got in. Once Ray got back at four thirty I went round to the Dobsons'. I stuck my head in the kitchen to warn them I was expecting a client at five.

He was early. The stench of cigarette smoke hit me as I opened the door. He had a base-ball jacket over his uniform.

'Come in.'

Once he'd sat down I recited the bald facts as I'd uncovered them. I described following Tina from home to the Worcester Hotel. Tina registering as Mrs Peters, as she'd done several times before. The man joining her, leaving after an hour, Tina coming out later. I had photographs of each of them outside the hotel, nothing of them together.

'Shit.' He made as if to rise, then slumped back into his seat. 'Shit.'

'I'm sorry,' I ventured.

His jaw muscles clenched as he bit down hard. His fist pressing against his mouth. 'You know anything about this guy?'

'No,' I answered.

'I asked her,' he said, 'last night, whether anything had happened, what she'd done with the day. She'd been bored, she said, she'd rung her mum to arrange to go over

92

for the weekend. She was thinking of taking up another class, something to do. Shit.'

I passed him the photos of the man. Jimmy looked at the top one, his hand trembling.

'Do you know him?'

He shook his head. Breathed in sharply and sat upright. 'OK, can I take this?'

'They're yours.'

'And the money?'

I passed him the bill, he read it and drew out some notes from his pocket. 'There's sixty there, I can pay the rest next week.'

'Fine. I'll give you a receipt.'

He brushed the offer aside. He stood up, his whole body tense. I wanted to make it better but this wasn't a child with a grazed knee. Jimmy and Tina were adults and only they could sort this out, for better or worse. I passed him the photo he'd given me of Tina. I felt a flicker of fear for her. 'If you and Tina want any help...' I held out a leaflet from Relate. I keep a pile to give out. If I have to go around uncovering betrayal and adultery then at least I can hand out a lifeline to those couples who might not want instant divorce.

He snorted and stuck his hands firmly in his pockets.

'I'll see you out.'

He bounded up the stairs to the door.

'Hey,' I said, as he made to leave. He turned to me, his face taut, his eyes bright with anger.

What could I say? Don't do anything daft? 'I'm sorry.'

He wheeled away to the van at the gate, hands fumbling in his pocket for his cigarettes.

CHAPTER TEN

It was Tuesday of the following week. Temperatures had plummeted and black ice glassed the roads and pavements. I was in the office with the little convector heater blasting out hot air. The phone rang. I picked it up, automatically pulling pen and paper towards me. Agnes introduced herself.

'I wanted to speak to you about Lily,' she said. 'They've moved her. When I went to visit yesterday Mrs Valley-Brown saw me. They transferred her during the night.'

'To Kingsfield?'

'Yes.'

'Oh, I am sorry.' I waited for her to carry on. I sympathised with Agnes but what was she ringing me for? Was I the only person she could tell? I had a sudden chill as I imagined Agnes becoming dependent on me, investing me with the role of social worker as she herself became less independent, ringing me in the night, turning up on the doorstep...

'I expect you're wondering why I rang you?' she said, wiping out my fantasy. 'You see, I'd like to hire you again.'

'But why?'

'To find out more. That probably sounds a little feeble,' she said, 'but I still feel ... I can't shake...' Emotion prevented her continuing. I gave her a few seconds.

'Perhaps I'd better come round,' I suggested.

'Or I could come to you,' she rallied.

'No, I've got the car. I'll be there in a quarter of an hour.'

I squirted de-icer over the car window inside and out and created streaky gaps to peer through. The steering wheel was so cold it made my fingers ache. Other people bought steering wheel covers or driving gloves. Somehow there was always something higher up my list like new shoes for Maddie or getting the vacuum cleaner fixed.

Agnes had tea already made and laid out

in the front room. I took my coat off and sat down. I motioned to the teapot. 'It's been a while since I've seen a tea cosy.'

'It keeps it warm,' she said. 'It's not leaf tea, mind. I went over to tea bags as soon as they came in. All that mess, clogging the plug hole.' She smiled. She poured the tea and passed me mine.

'So?' I invited her to talk.

'You probably think I'm foolish, throwing good money after bad. Maybe so. I'm just so worried about Lily. I want to make sure she's all right.'

Apart from having dementia, I thought to myself. 'What's actually worrying you?' I asked. 'What do you think might be wrong?'

'They've rushed her into hospital, it's all so sudden. Too sudden. Just like with her illness. Why all the hurry?' She looked at me, eyes dark blue, frank. 'I'm not an illogical person. I don't like the way things are happening so quickly. I can't stop worrying about Lily. I'm making myself ill with it.' Her eyes glittered but she made no move to wipe them.

I set down my tea. 'Lily's ill. She's deteriorating. Pretty soon the Lily you know will have gone. And sometime later there'll be her physical death. It could be this that you're anxious about.'

'I have thought about that.' As she spoke tears trailed down her cheeks, catching and spreading along the network of creases. 'And I have tried to accept it. But there are these inconsistencies,' she said. She stood up and went over to get a tissue from the box on the sideboard. 'Alzheimer's doesn't progress so quickly, read any of the books. Two months ago Lily was at home, leading an independent life. Now she's in hospital, transferred there in the middle of the night. It doesn't add up. And that Dr Goulden, he's been funny with me. He more or less accused me of taking Lily's tablets.'

'What?'

'He apologised later. It was yesterday. After talking to Mrs Valley-Brown I went to gather Lily's things together. I was doing that when I heard people arguing in the corridor. It was Mrs Knight and Dr Goulden. He was shout-ing something about checking the bottles, accounting for everything. I couldn't hear her reply, then he said he knew it had been the middle of the night, except he used very strong language, but it was still her respon-sibility.' Dr Goulden seemed to have a pro-pensity for bawling out his female colleagues.

'Then they came into the room. He asked me what the hell I thought I was doing and told me to put everything back. Mrs Knight explained I was a friend and when he realised I wasn't another resident his manner changed. I think she was quite embarrassed, she went crimson. Well, he explained that Lily's tablets hadn't been returned to the medicine cupboard as they always were in between doses. He said it had probably been overlooked in the commotion. He asked me to empty out the bags I was filling so he could check I'd not packed them by mistake.'

Agnes leant forward and replenished our cups. 'I knew I hadn't and I told him so but he insisted. He said it was a serious offence for drugs to be unaccounted for. So I tipped it all out and he rifled through it and thanked me and apologised for any confusion, as he put it, then off he went. I suppose they worry about somebody taking the wrong drugs.'

'Lily hadn't taken them with her?'

'No. She didn't take anything at all. Just the night clothes she was wearing. Mrs Valley-Brown said she had been extremely distressed and they'd found it impossible to calm her. She was already on tranquillisers, she didn't respond to the sedative they tried and they didn't want to give her anything stronger.'

I wondered whether Dr Goulden had

done anything about Lily's medicine in the week since we'd seen him. The situation certainly hadn't stabilised and Lily had obviously become worse. But again I came back to the fact that I was no doctor. I might be able to uncover signs of negligence if Goulden had ignored our concerns and had not been monitoring Lily, but I thought that was about the best I could hope for.

'There's a limit to what I can do.' I put my cup down. 'One or two visits to Kingsfield, see Lily, perhaps find a friendly staff member to ask about her case. Try to establish what happened the night she was transferred and whether Goulden had failed to see she was getting worse. Even if we could prove that and made an official complaint there's no guarantee anything would come of it. Did you talk to Charles about getting a second opinion?'

'He said he'd consider it. I think he thought I was overreacting. Charles doesn't like to rock the boat.'

'Well, now she's at the hospital she will be seeing a different doctor. It might be better for her.'

'Yes,' she nodded. 'Can you go tomorrow?'
'Yes. With you?'
'I can't,' she began to load the tray, 'I've a

funeral in the morning.'

'How about the afternoon?'

'The chiropodist.'

I was surprised that she wouldn't be re-arranging the routine appointment to visit her friend. She seemed a little ashamed too, refused to meet my eye as she busied herself with the tea things. Maybe she'd waited months for the chiropodist to come; perhaps she'd drop to the bottom of the list if she cancelled.

'All right. So I just turn up.'

'They call it the Marion Unit. If you could take some things for her. I've sorted out the essentials for now, things she might need immediately. There's a bag in the hall.'

'OK. So, I'll go along tomorrow. We can always visit together after that and I'll see if I can arrange for us to meet the consultant.'

'Yes,' she said, without much enthusiasm. Dr Goulden's tantrum had probably put her off the profession altogether.

I had a swim at lunchtime, followed by a disappointing shower. Cold. More of a dribble than a shower really. There was lots of talk about what super new facilities hosting the Commonwealth Games would bring to the region but as far as I could remember the pools were to be somewhere over in

Wigan and I doubted whether the showers at Withington Baths were even on the list of works. People said the Games would bring jobs and investment – it sounded great but how come we'd been the only city actually to bid for them? Was there something that they weren't telling us? Agnes' news had clouded my day and my cynicism was showing.

Kingsfield was originally built on the out-skirts of the city, far enough away to protect the citizens from the 'lunatics' in the asylum. Since then the city had grown and now the hospital and its grounds nestled between a private housing development and an indus-trial estate.

It was a vast Victorian edifice, all red-brick pomp, three storeys high with wings at either end. On top of the central entrance a small bell tower rose. The gardens to the front were mainly converted to parking, and signs pointed the way to the Plasma Re-search Centre, Service Supplies, Speech Therapy, Artificial Limb Centre and the Marion Unit (psycho-geriatric).

I went through the main entrance, which was all green and black tiles and tasteful indoor plant features, and was directed down the main corridor for some way. It was huge, the size of any major infirmary. In its heyday it must have housed hundreds of people. Where had they all gone? Being cared for in the community, or not, if one believed half of the reports being issued.

I was directed along a corridor to the right and then out and across a courtyard. The gardening budget had obviously been cut. Untended beds and containers sprouted dead grass and frost-hardy weeds.

The Marion Unit was a modern, two-storey concrete rectangle with a large grey metal triangle leaping upwards from the flat roof. As if the architect had tried to redeem the utter lack of imagination by plonking a concept on top.

Inside and immediately opposite the heavy glass entrance doors there was a reception area with a glass booth and a small office. Three women, one in uniform, were chatting there. I approached and the huddle broke up. A woman in a smart grey wool dress, her name badge identifying her as Mrs Li, greeted me.

I asked if I could visit Lily Palmer and explained that she'd been admitted on Monday night. She told me to take a seat for a moment.

She went into the office and used the

phone. I sat in the waiting area. Some attempt had been made to make it comfortable. The seats were padded foam, there were a couple of inoffensive prints on the wall and a large drinks machine. There were magazines on the table here too, along with leaflets about the Alzheimer's Disease Society, 'Caring for an Elderly Person' and 'How to Stay Warm in Winter'.

After, a couple of minutes a young nurse appeared from one of the doors to the waiting room and took me through to the dayroom. It was large and brightly lit, with a television at the far end. Low tables and chairs were clustered here and there, as well as a couple of ordinary ones with cards and dominoes on them.

There were quite a lot of people in the room. Some sat quietly, withdrawn, others muttered or sang to themselves. One man was shouting. The room stank of potpourri and there was a stale, sour smell that it couldn't quite mask.

I followed the nurse briskly through the lounge to the corridor at the bottom. I glanced into the rooms as we passed by. Most seemed to have four beds in. Some beds were occupied.

'How's she been?' I asked the nurse.

'Fine,' she spoke with an Irish accent, 'just fine. There's a lot they can do with the medication. She's a bit sleepy with it but a lot calmer.'

'Who decides on the treatment?'

'Dr Montgomery, he's the consultant. Have you not seen him yet?'

'No.'

She paused outside one of the doors, knocked, then without waiting for a reply she opened the door and we went in.

Lily sat in a chair next to her bed, eyes half-shut. She wore a hospital-issue night-gown and a blanket round her knees.

'I've brought her some things of her own.' I turned to the nurse, uncertain whether Lily could hear me.

'They can go in the locker. They might go walking. Some of them lose track, they've no sense of personal possessions. There's noth-ing valuable, is there?' I shook my head. 'Do you hear that, Lily?' The nurse raised her voice. 'Here's someone to see you. They've brought your things. You can put them in your locker.'

Lily opened her eyes but they remained unfocused.

'I'll leave you then,' said the nurse. 'I'll be in the dayroom if you're needing anything.'

I pulled up a second chair and sat down. 'Hello, Lily. Agnes asked me to bring these for you.' There was no response. She gazed across the room, her glasses smeared and speckled with dirt. I placed the bag on her lap. She never moved. She didn't seem to be aware of it let alone the fact that I was there. I felt foolish. When she got up the bag would fall on the floor, she could trip over it and hurt herself.

'Shall I put it in your locker?' I reached over and put my hand on the bag. Swiftly Lily brought her hand up and gripped my wrist.

'Agnes won't come,' she said urgently.

'She couldn't,' I replied, 'not today. She had a funeral to go to and an appointment.'

'Won't come,' she repeated. 'Kingsfield. Nora came.' She let go of my wrist suddenly so I almost overbalanced. I sat down again.

'I'm sure Agnes will come as soon as she can,' I said, 'and I'll tell her Nora's been. Agnes is worried about you. She wants to know if you're all right. Is there anything you need?'

She closed her eyes. I sat waiting for her to open them but she'd gone to sleep. I took the bag and placed it on top of the locker.

In the dayroom the man was still shouting

and the Irish nurse was joking with a group of residents. I found the sister in charge, Sister Darling. I told her I wanted to talk to the consultant about Lily. Was I next of kin? A close relative? No. She apologised but Dr Montgomery could only see next of kin.

'Who is Mrs Palmer's closest relative?'

'Her son. But he's down in Devon.'

'Nevertheless he'll be informed of anything that matters. Perhaps you should talk to him. Are you related at all?'

'Just a friend,' I smiled. I didn't want to be questioned too closely. 'I'll speak to her son then.'

After the sweltering heat of the hospital the outside world felt arctic. I was shivering by the time I got into the car. I drove back along the dual carriageway and past Southern Cemetery. Lily would end up here. How long would the disease take to kill her? If it had come on more quickly than usual would it progress quickly too? And would that make it any easier on Lily or those who loved her? Impossible questions.

I cut through East Didsbury and up to Withington. At the office I switched on the heater and stomped around until it felt safe to take my coat off. I made a few notes about my visit, checked the answerphone and locked up. But I couldn't lock up so neatly my memories of that woman, alone in the hospital. Nor could I forget that momentary feeling I'd had that Agnes wasn't being quite straight with me.

CHAPTER ELEVEN

The wind had got up by late afternoon. Straight from the North Pole by the feel of it. My nose dripped and my eyes watered. I wrapped my scarf tighter round my face and struggled to school. The children hated it, whining all the way back about being freezing and stinging snow (meaning hail) and how itchy their hats were. I bought crumpets from the corner shop to celebrate our return to base camp.

The house was like an ice-box. I checked the central heating dial. It had stopped. The lights were on in the kitchen but the fridge wasn't working either. Or the toaster.

'I want my crumpet now,' demanded Maddie, bashing the washing machine controls with her fist.

'You'll get it as soon as I've sorted this

out,' I snapped.

'I hate you,' she retorted.

'You could come and help. We'll have to check the fuses in the cellar.'

She wheeled away disdainfully.

'I will,' piped up Tom.

'It'll all go dark for a bit,' I called after Maddie while I rooted around in the drawer for the torch.

Some brilliant thinker had actually labelled the fuses in the past so I could find the right one quickly. And, joy of joys, there was fuse wire on top of the fuse box. I switched off the mains and removed the fuse. It was burned through.

Solemnly Tom held the fuse while I measured a piece of wire in the light from the torch. I could hear Maddie shuffling on the cellar steps, wanting to be with us but not wanting to admit it.

'Maddie,' I said, 'could you hold the torch?'

'Why?'

'Then I can fix the new wire.'

Big sigh. She came down and took the torch. I fixed the fuse and replaced it, turned the power back on. Tom and Maddie ran upstairs to see if it worked.

Victory. Crumpets on, heating reset, oven warming up. I grabbed a crumpet and some tea. Then chopped vegetables up and slung them in a casserole with tinned butter beans and stock.

The evening paper had arrived. I picked it up and returned to the kitchen. It was warm now, smelled good. I closed the blinds, turned Digger out of my chair. Fifteen minutes' peace catching up on the local news would be just the job. I'd empty the washing machine first, a reminder to take it downstairs to dry later. I opened the door. Gallons of cold soapy water gushed over my feet and into the kitchen.

Ray came in cursing the weather. It had affected supplies of various materials and as a result he was laid off until further notice. The bright side, as far as I was concerned, was he'd be around to take his turn with the school run and the cooking. I didn't think it would be tactful to point it out at the time.

We'd just finished eating when the bell rang and Sheila introduced herself. She was older than I'd expected, with a grey bob and wire-rimmed specs. We talked first in the kitchen. Explained how things were organised, rent, bills, shared use of the kitchen, the washer and drier and so on. There were few rules; no smoking and clean up after yourself being the most important.

Sheila grinned. 'Tell me about it. I'm sharing with two students at the moment. The mess. I got it through the university – I'm doing a degree course. I'd no idea there'd be so little choice. I might have been able to stand it at eighteen but...' She looked over at Tom and Maddie, who were silently fighting over a chair. 'I've two boys myself actually.'

'How old are they?' piped up Maddie.

'Nineteen and twenty-two. Dominic's up at St Andrew's studying law and Peter's in India backpacking.'

I wondered whether Peter and Dominic would descend on Sheila in between terms. And what had happened to the family home? Sold, she later told me, to pay off her husband's debts. His business had failed, spectacularly. And then the marriage failed, too.

'I'm five,' announced Maddie.

'I'm four,' said Tom.

Would she be tempted to interfere with how we raised the children? She seemed easy-going enough.

'Would you like to have a look at the rooms?' I suggested.

'Follow the leader, I'm leader,' shrieked Tom.

We filed upstairs to the first floor.

'Bathroom,' Ray pointed out, 'bath and shower. Sal's room, mine.'

'This is my room,' called Maddie.

'It's not just yours,' Tom proclaimed, 'it's mine as well.' Sheila tolerated a tour of the children's room and made all the right noises as they showed her their treasures. We climbed up the attic stairs. Digger lay sprawled on the landing.

'We've got a dog,' I said.

'He's called Digger,' said Tom.

'Do you like dogs?' Maddie asked.

'I like cats better,' Sheila replied diplomatically.

'He's Ray's dog,' I told her. 'I rescued him from the pound and then discovered I wasn't all that keen on dogs.'

'He's a great dog,' said Ray proudly.

Digger pricked his ears, opened his eyes and beamed love at his master. His tail thumped the ground. We stepped over him to show Sheila the rooms. 'Bedroom here, loo in the middle, sitting room there.'

'You can shift them round,' said Ray.

'It's lovely,' said Sheila, 'all the sloping roofs, and you've kept the old fireplaces.'

'They work too,' I said. 'The windows are pretty poky but I think the owners ran out of money once they'd put the central heating in up here. We'll leave you to look round a bit,' I suggested. 'We'll be down in the kitchen.'

Downstairs Ray and I had a quick confab and agreed that we'd like her to move in if she was still keen. When she reappeared Ray asked her what she thought.

'It's lovely. I don't know if you're seeing other people.'

'No,' I said, 'it's yours if you want to move in.'

'Oh, yes.' Her hands flew to her mouth as she stifled an exclamation. 'Oh, it's such a relief.' For a moment I thought she was going to go all weepy on us but she took a deep breath and beamed. We agreed that she'd bring her stuff on Friday and sorted out a time when we'd be in.

Everybody was happy and a third adult paying into the rent and bills would ease the financial strain that Ray and I had been under for the last few months.

That evening Ray did bedtime and I put my feet up, sank into one of my books. When the phone rang I thought it was going to be Agnes but it was my friend Diane.

'I need a good natter,' she said. 'This weather is driving me round the bend. Do you know what I ate for tea last night? All because I couldn't face walking to the shops –

tinned pilchards, pitta bread and limp celery.'

'Probably very nutritious,' I said.

'It was revolting. Anyway I had to go out today. I ran out of biscuits.'

Diane is a foodie. Any food. Health food, junk food. And most of all sweet food. She's also fat, her word for it. She gave up dieting in her teens and now she's completely comfortable about her size. Big and bold about it, she wears bright, patterned clothes which she runs up on an old treadle sewing machine.

We arranged to meet up at our usual local for a drink the following night.

While I was in phone mode I rooted out Agnes' number and rang her. I told her I'd seen Lily, passed the clothes on, that she'd been fairly sleepy. I didn't go into exactly what Lily had said, I felt it might be less upsetting to Agnes if I told her face to face that Lily felt abandoned.

'I asked about seeing Dr Montgomery, the consultant, but they only allow next of kin. Have you spoken to Lily's son?'

'Charles? No.'

'You could find out what he's been told and see if he's any plans to see Dr Montgomery. It might be worth asking if he'll nominate you as another close contact, with him being so far away.'

'Yes. I'll try him tonight.'

'I can pop round tomorrow and fill you in on my visit and you can tell me what he says then.'

Thursday dawned with a layer of snow two inches deep. Rare for Manchester, though the outlying hills get their fair share. The kids were delirious, out in wellies, coats and pyjamas before breakfast, scraping snow together to make a snowman. They weren't making much progress. I went out and gave them a hand – showed them how to roll a snowball round, make it bigger and bigger. The snow was just right, made that delicious squeaking sound when we squashed it. We created a very short snowman complete with pebble eyes, a carrot nose and a baseball hat.

Ray took Maddie and Tom to school and was busy in the cellar when I set off to see Agnes.

As soon as I was in the room she crossed to the sideboard, opened a drawer and took something out. She came over and handed me a bottle of tablets. 'I found these,' she said, 'Lily's tablets.'

'Where?'

'She has these little boots, fur-lined. They were inside one of them.'

'Do you think she'd hidden them?'

Agnes shrugged. 'I don't know. She kept the boots near the bed, like spare slippers, the bottle could have been knocked off. I didn't find them till I was sorting through her other things.'

'Dr Goulden will be relieved.'

'I don't want you to tell him.'

'Why?'

'Look.' She pulled another bottle from her pocket. 'These are the same thing, thioridazine – I had them for a while myself – but Lily's are different, the colour and the markings.'

I took a tablet out of each bottle. True, they were different colours, Lily's were a pale yellow while Agnes' were white. 'They could be a different dosage,' I said, 'or made by different manufacturers.' I looked again at the labels on the bottles. Both said they were 25 mg. 'They are the same strength but as far as I know doctors deal with different drug companies and some use cheaper versions of the more famous brands. I'm sure that's all it is, the same thing from different places.'

'Can you check,' Agnes asked, 'that they are what they say?'

'You think they might have made a mistake with the prescription?'

'It's possible.'

I put the tablets back and screwed up the lids. 'It would explain why Goulden was so anxious when they went missing. And why Lily got worse. Maybe that's it – an awful mistake and he'd only just realised... I'll have them analysed. I think I know someone who could get them into a lab.' I slipped the bottle into my coat pocket.

Agnes sat down. I began to tell her about my visit to Kingsfield. 'Lily didn't say very much. The medication she's on makes her sleepy. But she mentioned you.'

'She did?' Pleasure lit her eyes.

'Yes, she was worried you wouldn't visit. Perhaps she's aware it's harder for you to get to. She said Agnes won't come. I explained you were busy and told her I was sure you'd come when you could.'

Agnes nodded, her face slightly flushed.

'Oh, and she said Nora'd been to see her.'

Agnes started. 'Nora. What Nora?'

'I'm sure she said Nora. After she talked about you not coming she said Nora came.'

Bright red spots bloomed on Agnes' cheeks. 'There's no Nora,' she said emphatically, 'she's talking nonsense.'

'Perhaps it's one of the other patients,' I suggested.

Agnes toyed with her brooch, a gold spray of lily of the valley. I wondered whether she wore them to satisfy that nervous tic, like people who are lost without earrings to fidget with or those who keep their hair long so they can twirl it round their fingers.

'The staff seem very nice,' I broke the silence, 'although it feels much more like a hospital than Homelea. Lily's in a room with three other beds but I didn't meet any of the other patients.'

'Yes,' she said. She gazed at the flames that were licking the fake coal. She seemed a million miles away. Unlike the determined woman who insisted I take the case.

'Agnes, is everything all right?'

'Yes.' She shook herself from her reverie.

'Did you speak to Charles?'

'Yes. Mrs Valley-Brown rang him on Tuesday to let him know about the transfer. She told him there was no cause for alarm, that Lily had become difficult to manage and the care she needed could best be provided at the hospital. He didn't think there was anything untoward about the haste.'

'What about naming you as a nearby contact?'

She sighed. 'He's coming up tomorrow to visit and he'll see Dr Montgomery then. He said he'd ask about it. Charles has no objection.'

What should my next move be? I should probably go back to Homelea and try to find out more about the night of Lily's move and Dr Goulden's outburst over the tablets. I could also accompany Agnes to Kingsfield, chat to the staff about Lily's condition.

'When are you going to see her?' I asked.

'I'm not sure,' said Agnes. 'If Charles is going tomorrow I may leave it till Saturday.' She was less than keen.

'We could go up together,' I suggested. 'I don't know what time would suit me yet but I can ring you.'

'Yes.' She rose from her chair.

'Meanwhile I'll pop into Homelea and see what I can find out.'

She saw me to the door. Said goodbye. I was beginning to wonder about the wisdom of working for Agnes. She blew hot and cold about the case; urging me to get the tablets checked one minute and going all vague and dreamy on me the next. I felt she was being evasive with me whereas I'd originally found her to be forthright and honest. Was it a false first impression or had something happened to change her?

CHAPTER TWELVE

Diane was settled with a drink in our favourite corner when I arrived at the pub. It'd been our watering hole for years and to date the brewery had resisted the temptation to turn a perfectly pleasant local boozer into some theme pub for the younger end of the market. Consequently it was quiet enough for us to have a good chat and you could always get a seat. The beer was good too. Creamy Boddies kept just cool enough by the landlord.

I bought a pint and joined Diane.

'You look brighter than you sounded,' I remarked.

She raised her eyebrows. 'Good news.'

'What?'

She grinned.

'Go on!'

'I've got a show,' she beamed.

'What! Where?'

'The Cornerhouse.'

'Oh, Diane.'

'Three weeks, first-floor gallery.'

'Brilliant.'

'And...' She put her glass down.

'There's more?'

'A tour of the North West after.'

'Oh, wow! When did you hear?' I squirmed with pleasure.

'This morning. The woman from The Cornerhouse rang. They want it up in October.'

'Fame and fortune.'

'Well, fame maybe. I won't make anything unless it sells.'

'Course it will. They'll be falling over each other to buy you. Trendy or what?'

'I'll have to get a serious haircut.'

'What?'

'Well, they all have haircuts, don't they, very stylish.'

'It's your prints they're after. Besides, what do you call that?' I signalled in the direction of Diane's blatant strawberry-coloured wedge.

'Go on!' she said.

'Well, it's hardly natural, is it? I'd say it was a pretty definite hairstyle.'

She giggled.

I shared her delight at the news. She deserved some recognition. I loved her prints – silk screen and batik – but she barely made a living out of them. We talked some more about the exhibition and the work it would involve before the conversation turned to me.

'I'm fairly busy,' I said, 'but I don't know how long it will last. It could just fizzle out.' I explained in general the job Agnes was asking me to do. I always confide in Diane; I never name names and I trust her not to go blabbing about what she's heard.

'There are a few weird things about it all, her rapid decline and this business with the pills, but it may all be perfectly innocent.'

'And why anyway?' said Diane.

'Why what?'

'Why would anyone want to make this woman ill? Who benefits? Hey, maybe you should check the will – has she recently changed it in favour of the nursing home? Does her family know? That could be it. Sign on the dotted line and bingo – soon as she pops her clogs they get their hands on the money.'

I laughed. It was a preposterous idea. Nevertheless I would find out who were the beneficiaries if Lily died.

'Anyway,' I said, 'if you wanted to kill someone there's quicker ways, aren't there? More certain too. Especially someone frail. A serious fall when she's alone in her room, perhaps.'

'Ah, but sudden death,' said Diane.

'They'd have to do a post-mortem.'

'On an eighty-five-year-old? They'd probably get away with it as long as the GP was satisfied it was natural cause of death. Besides she's not dead and as I said, it could all be above board and I'll be filling in the Housing Benefit forms again next week if something else doesn't turn up.'

We carried on till closing time, then parted company, riding our bikes away in different directions. The snow had turned to watery brown fudge along the pavements and most of the roads were clear. As I put my bike away I noticed the snowman was still there though the grass was no longer white.

The dog down the road was barking steadily on, liking the sound of its own voice. Didn't its owners ever get sick of the noise? 'Shut up!' I yelled as I put my key in the lock. It never even paused for breath.

I think it was only the fact that I'd been there before that prevented Mrs Knight, the matron at Homelea, from telling me to bog off.

I knocked on her office door and she called for me to come in.

'I'd just like a word about Mrs Palmer,' I said, closing the door behind me. 'I was so sorry to hear about her transfer. I've been to see her and she doesn't seem at all well. What happened?'

She opened her mouth and half rose. Then thought better of it. 'Please sit down.' She gestured to the spare chair.

'As you know, Mrs Valley-Brown was happy to have Mrs Palmer here as long as there was no adverse effect on our other residents. But I'm afraid we were getting quite a lot of wandering, she was increasingly restless and then she was suffering with night incontinence much more frequently. Things became very difficult on Sunday night. Mrs Palmer was extremely distressed and failed to respond at all to the medication we gave her. She became aggressive and was obviously suffering from delusions.' She spoke calmly and quietly, using the sort of soothing tones reserved for bad news. And she never smiled.

'What sort of delusions?'

'Paranoid fantasies. She was being poisoned, someone was stealing all her things. These aren't uncommon. We felt she was a danger to herself if not to others. Dr Goulden was called out and he had her admitted to Kingsfield.'

'Couldn't she have gone into a residential nursing home instead?'

'Dr Goulden felt Kingsfield was the most

appropriate alternative. There she'll get a full assessment and a detailed care plan. The psycho-geriatrician may recommend a private nursing home if her behaviour can be managed with medication. After all, it was her failure to respond to the drug treatment we were using that was most worrying and the doctor didn't want to prescribe anything else on top of that in case of side effects.'

'That was the thioridazine?'

Mrs Knight nodded. 'Yes, and we'd tried a sedative as well but nothing worked.'

'It was the thioridazine that went missing?' I asked.

'Sorry?' She looked shocked.

'Miss Donlan said there's been a row about missing tablets. Dr Goulden as good as accused her of stealing them.'

'I think there's been a misunderstanding,' she said. 'Dr Goulden was a little brusque. We have to account carefully for all the drugs here and he felt there'd been some laxity. Neither of us realised it at the time but they'd been returned by one of the care assistants.'

She was a lousy liar. A muscle twitched in her cheek and she couldn't meet my eye.

'Then why couldn't Dr Goulden find them on the Tuesday when Miss Donlan was here?'

'The silly girl had put them on the wrong shelf,' she replied.

'Is it common practice to allow all the staff access to the medicine store?'

She swallowed. 'No, but there are occasions when we may have to do that, when other priorities take precedence.'

Before I could quiz her any more there was a tapping sound at the door and it opened.

'Mrs Valley-Brown,' said Mrs Knight, 'this is ... I'm sorry, I didn't get your name?'

'Kilkenny,' I said, 'Sal Kilkenny.'

'We've been having a chat about Mrs Palmer.'

'Hello.' She came further into the room. She wore a cherry-red wool suit, matching lipstick and piles of jewellery. Her hair was streaked a dozen different shades and gently curled. She was probably in her fifties though it was hard to tell. Her face was plastered with thick orange foundation though she wore only a trace of eye make-up. No one on earth had ever had skin that colour. It looked like jaundice mixed with sunburn. 'How is Mrs Palmer?' She smiled. The red lipstick gave her teeth a yellow cast.

'Quite subdued,' I said.

'They'll do their very best for her there,'

she said. 'Dr Montgomery is excellent, isn't he, Gail?'

Mrs Knight nodded.

'It was all so quick,' I began. Hoping to plant a few doubts in one of their minds.

'It may seem like that,' said Mrs Knight, 'but the dementia may have been developing for many months before she came to us.'

I'd been here before. 'It was more sudden than most, though, wasn't it? She was only here a few weeks and now she's in hospital.'

'We are dealing with people here,' said Mrs Valley-Brown, 'such a variety. You know yourself how a common cold can lay one person low but only give another a sniffle. I think in a case like this we must remember to look at the individual, not just the illness.' She smiled, tilting her head on one side in an attempt to look sympathetic, I think. So where did the platitudes get me? Yes, it was a bit quick but c'est la vie!

Before I could say anything else she turned back to the matron. 'Now, Gail, about Mrs Jarvis, I can come back later if you...'

'No, we're finished.' Mrs Knight stood up, a signal for me to leave.

As I left, my hands curled round the bottle of drugs in my pocket. The bottle that Mrs Knight claimed had been put back. Mrs

126

Knight the liar.

I drove to Moira's that afternoon, on spec. I'd done a steady thirty lengths at the baths and it wasn't far from there to her house in Fallowfield. I knew she sometimes got a break in between morning and afternoon surgery if she didn't have too many home visits.

Her car was in the drive.

'Yes?' she barked before the door was fully open. 'Sal! Come in, kettle's boiled.'

'I've brought the books back,' I said.

'Any use?'

'Yeah, gave me the background.'

'Tea, coffee, herbals?'

'Coffee, please.'

She spooned coffee into mugs, poured in water. 'Was it acute – the confusion?'

'No, well, apparently not. Just pretty quick. But the woman's even worse now. Been transferred to Kingsfield.'

'Case over? Milk, sugar?'

'Yes, no. Yes milk, no sugar. Case not over, not quite. The client still wants further enquiries. That's the other reason I called.'

Moira handed me a mug. Cradled her own in her hand, leaning against the work surface.

I put the coffee down, pulled the bottle from my pocket. 'My client thinks there may be some problem with these.' I handed it to Moira. She read the label.

'They don't look the same as her own,' I explained. 'I told her different companies probably used different packaging.'

'Can do,' Moira agreed.

'But if I could get them analysed. We think there could be some mistake; it would explain a lot.' I paused. Would Moira offer or would I have to beg? I sipped coffee.

'Take a few days,' she said, 'even if you did have access to a lab.' Only the way she chewed her lip gave away the wind-up.

'Moira!'

'All right. Just don't make a habit of it.'

Ray was collecting the children so I had the whole afternoon to play with. I drove up to Rusholme and bought some authentic ingredients for a good curry. Lady's fingers and a whole bouquet of coriander – a far cry from the sprigs on sale at the supermarket. I stocked up on spices too, and a selection of pickles, chutneys and ready-made sauces.

I drove along to Longsight Market. Open-air stalls selling cheap clothes, household goods, gadgets and fabric. I bought some woolly tights and a corduroy pinafore dress for Maddie, and some cheap videotapes. I spent ten minutes hovering over a printed silk blouse before putting it back. I'd never get the chance to wear it. It was nightclub gear really, or the sort of thing for balmy nights on foreign holidays. Fat chance.

I dropped things off at home and gathered up my library books.

Spent a delicious hour browsing. Came away with a Frances Fyfield, a Walter Mosley, a James Lee Burke and the latest Minette Walters – well, the latest to reach the library shelves. Bliss. It was five when I got back home.

The police were waiting to see me.

CHAPTER THIRTEEN

I felt guilty. They knew I'd taken the tablets. Homelea had complained about me.

I took the police officers into the kitchen. Ray made himself scarce and went to join the children in the lounge.

There were two of them, plainclothes. A thick-set man with blue-black hair and very white skin, and a younger woman with a dark brown ponytail and a horsey face.

'I'm Detective Inspector Crawshaw,' said the man, 'and this is Detective Sergeant Bell.'

She flipped open her notepad. He established my name, address and occupation. Not a twitch when I said I was a private investigator.

'What's it all about?' I asked.

'We're investigating a serious crime and we think you may be able to help us with our enquiries. We'd like to ask you a few questions.'

He'd obviously done the public relations training. Lots of eye contact, a direct approach yet still managing to ignore my question.

'Do you know a Mr James Achebe?'

Oh, no. My guts clenched. Something was terribly wrong. A serious crime, they'd said.

'Yes, he's … he was a client.'

'When was this?'

'I finished that job last week.'

'And what was the nature of the work you did for him?'

'I guarantee confidentiality to my clients.'

'Yes, but in this situation,' he snapped, momentarily losing it. Then he reeled back in the modern management style. 'I'm sure you appreciate that there are certain situations where the right of client confidentiality no longer takes precedence.'

'Yes,' I said, 'but seeing as I don't know what this situation is, what this serious crime is or who might have committed it I'm hardly in a position to judge really, am I?'

He sighed briskly. Tried another approach. 'When did you last see Mr Achebe?'

I thought back. 'Thursday last week.'

'A week yesterday,' he glanced at his watch and did the arithmetic, 'the twenty-fourth?' I could never do that. I hadn't got a watch with a date on for a start.

'Yes.'

'And you've not seen him since?'

'No.'

'Nor spoken to him on the phone?'

'No.'

'Has he communicated with you in any way? Sent letters, left messages?'

'No, nothing.' I tried to keep the defensive note from my voice but I was beginning to, feel under suspicion myself.

Ray appeared at the kitchen door, the kids leaning close to him. Eyes agog at the police in the kitchen.

'We're going for chips,' said Ray. 'You?' I nodded.

'He's not a policeman,' said Tom scornfully, 'he hasn't got a hat.' Ray ushered them out.

'We need to know the nature of the job you did for Mr Achebe.'

'But I've already—'

He interrupted. 'You should be aware that Mr Achebe is being held in connection with enquiries into the death of his wife, Tina Achebe.'

'Oh, Jesus!' Tina, slight and smart in the check jacket. Jimmy, his whole body tense as he heard about her rendezvous at the hotel. 'Oh, no. When did this happen? How did she...?' A gunshot wound to the head? Or maybe suicide? Devastated by Jimmy's new-found knowledge, wrists emptying in the bath, tablets by the bed, feet dangling.

'Why did James Achebe hire you?'

I took a deep breath. 'He was worried about his wife, about Tina. He thought she was keeping something from him.'

'How do you mean?'

'She wasn't at home when he thought she would be. She lied about whether she'd been in or out. That sort of thing.'

'Go on.'

'I watched the house. One day I followed her. She went to town. To a hotel. She booked into a room. A man joined her there.'

'And?'

I shrugged. 'They were there for an hour

132

or so then he left. A while later she left as well. Went home.'

'When was this?'

'Wednesday, the day before I saw Jimmy, Wednesday the twenty-third.'

The doorbell rang. I jerked in my seat with the shock of it. Feeling ridiculous I excused myself for a minute.

It was Sheila, complete with a blue Manchester Van Hire van stuffed full of gear.

'Sheila, I'm sorry,' I blurted, 'I'm in the middle of something. I'll have to leave you to it. Ray should be back soon, he's just gone for chips.'

'Don't worry,' she grinned. 'Malcolm's giving me a hand. We'll just get on with it.' Said Malcolm emerged from the far side of the van and gave a friendly wave.

Back in the kitchen Sergeant Bell had obviously been checking her notes. She riffled through her notebook to find her place. Inspector Crawshaw took up where we'd left off.

'You last saw Mr Achebe on the Thursday, the day after you'd followed his wife to this hotel?'

'Yes. I had to tell him what I'd found out.'

'How did he take it?'

'Like anybody would. He was hurt, upset.'

'Did he give any indication of what he was going to do about it?'

'No.' Jimmy hadn't threatened to kill her. Something I'd heard so many times in marital work. 'He was hurt, like I say. She was very important to him. When he came to see me, I got the impression he really wanted the marriage to work. Not like some people who've already had enough and just want proof for ending the relationship. When did she die? Was she killed or was it suicide?'

'We're not in possession of all the facts yet. Mrs Achebe's body was discovered yesterday morning. Suicide is most unlikely. The man you saw meet Mrs Achebe, can you describe him?'

Murder then. 'I've got a photograph – well, I gave the prints to Jimmy ... to Mr Achebe.'

'And the negatives?'

'I've got them at the office.'

'We'd like to take them away with us.'

'Now?'

'Yes.'

'It's round the corner,' I said, 'walking distance.'

He stood up. 'Right, then.' Sergeant Bell closed her book.

We walked along the road and met Ray, Maddie and Tom coming the other way. I felt embarrassed. Maddie ran to me.

'Mummy, Mummy. We've got chips.'

'I know. I won't be long. I'm just popping round to the office for something.'

'Can I come?' Maddie clamoured.

'No, you get the chips ready for me. Sheila's moving her stuff in.' I thought she'd throw a tantrum but the news of Sheila defused it and she turned to Ray.

The police followed me downstairs in silence. I retrieved the negatives from the file in the cabinet and handed them over. There was just one strip of shots. 'There's a couple of Tina and some of the man.'

Crawshaw held the strip up to the light and squinted, grunted. Slipped them into their envelope and pocketed them.

I walked back home in more awkward silence. It was a relief to say goodbye to the police.

'We'll be in touch if there are any further questions,' Inspector Crawshaw said.

Inside I fielded questions from the children about the police visit, ate my chips and tried to be welcoming to Sheila. What did she think of Manchester?

'Oh, I love it. I was down in Bury St Edmunds before, small town, so it's a complete change. I love the theatre and the galleries.' Flipping heck, when had I last been to either? 'And there's some superb concerts. I've been to the Royal Northern College a few times. There's such a lot going on I could spend all my time going out if I'd the money. I never expected it'd be like this.'

'Still thought we were in clogs and shawls?'

She laughed. 'Well, not quite. But, the rain, I can't believe it rains as much as it does, I thought that was part of the myth too.'

'No, that bit's true.' I sorted my remaining chips into edible and not. The ones I rejected were mainly those vicious little sharp bits designed to choke you. 'People don't realise. It's like when they were laying the tram lines. The firm that got the contract were outsiders. About a year after they'd laid it all the lines on Moseley Street started coming unstuck. They had to do it all again. Claimed they'd no idea it would rain so much.'

'Oh, that's awful.'

'And when the Velodrome first went up the roof leaked. Probably be the new Concert Hall next,' I said.

'I hope not,' she said, 'I intend to be a regular there.'

'On a student grant?'

'An occasional regular, then.'

Later I rooted out the evening paper. Tina Achebe was the main story, whole front page. Despite all the 'Gunchester' stories a murder is still big news in the city.

There was a photo of the house in Levens-hulme, quotes from a neighbour who had heard arguments on the Wednesday night and Thursday morning and had alerted the police when she couldn't get an answer from the house. The report said there were signs of a violent struggle but there was no detail about the cause of death. There was a grainy photograph of Tina and Jimmy posing form-ally in front of some blossom trees. Where did they get the photo from? No charges had been brought, the report said, but Mr Achebe was assisting police with their enquiries.

I had a bath, tried to relax. All the while images of Tina and Jimmy churned round my mind. And I struggled to convince myself that whatever had happened I couldn't be held to blame. I'd just been doing my job. There'd never been any atmosphere of vio-lence around Jimmy. I wouldn't have taken the work on if I'd sensed anything like that.

It was a losing battle. In bed I lay awake far into the night waiting for exhaustion to release me.

CHAPTER FOURTEEN

Birdsong. A note of cheer on a cold March morning. Then I remembered Tina. Dragged myself out of bed and down to breakfast.

Sheila was there, finding her way round the kitchen. I didn't think it was fair to confide in her. I'd passed off the police call of the previous evening as routine enquiries.

I had promised Agnes we'd call at Kingsfield but I needed to check if Ray could look after Maddie. We often did separate things at the weekends, each of us only responsible for our own child.

Tom and Maddie were glued to Saturday morning television. I asked them where Ray was. After three goes Tom managed to disengage long enough to answer. 'He's taken Digger for a walk.' I'd have to wait.

They arrived back an hour later. Digger, with mud up to his belly, stank to high heaven. Ray shut him in the kitchen.

'Can you look after Maddie for a couple of hours?'

'Sure, when? I said I'd take Tom over to my mother's.'

'Nowish. I just need to ring this woman up and check.' I got through to Agnes. She was ill.

'Some sort of flu, I think,' she said. 'I'm really not up to it.'

'Shall we leave it till next week?'

'Oh, no. You go,' she urged me on. 'Please. See how she is.'

Flu? Funny how things kept cropping up to prevent Agnes from going to visit Lily.

The snow had gone completely now, leaving a residue of grime where it had trapped the city muck. The sky had a blank, bleak cast. Traffic was thick with Saturday shoppers and visitors.

At the hospital I had trouble parking. By the time I reached the Marion Unit I was feeling as grim as the weather.

Lily was in the dayroom pacing round. She was agitated, rubbing and wringing her hands and muttering to herself. She was smaller than I remembered, the curve in her spine emphasising her short stature. Her permed hair was dishevelled, a flat patch

139

near the crown showing a glimpse of scalp. She wore a plain blue long-sleeved dress and slippers.

The room was busy, fifteen or twenty people, perhaps some visitors. I could only see one nurse in the room, mopping up a spill in the far corner. Someone tapped me on the shoulder. I turned round. The man had wiry grey hair sprouting from head, nostrils and ears. Enormous eyebrows. Grand with age. His face was leathery, dotted with liver spots. He took my hand and beamed at me. His whole face alight. A cracking smile. I smiled back. He crushed me to him in a sudden bear hug. I smelt menthol and zinc and the starchy smell of unwashed hair. Just as swiftly he released me and walked away.

Lily had reached the far end of the room, near the bedrooms. I caught up with her and touched her on the arm. 'Lily, it's Sal Kilkenny, I came the other day. Agnes asked me to visit, see how you are.'

She glanced at me, her round face flushed. There were tiny beads of perspiration on her nose and her forehead. She pushed her glasses up her nose, looked all about her then took my arm and led me to her room. She stopped beside her bed. I stood awkwardly at her side.

140

'How are you?' Would she talk to me or not?

'I can't find George. I don't know what they've done with him.'

'George?'

'He's a good man. Mother says he's a good man. With prospects. Do you know,' she leant towards me conspiratorially, 'the Wetherbys have got a half-share in a pig.'

Her husband, George, he'd gone missing in action in the Second World War, the Far East. I tried to bring her back to the present.

'Charles came to see you yesterday, from Exeter.'

'Charles. What Charles?'

'Your son Charles.'

She gasped. 'I haven't got a son. I'm not married yet. What sort of a girl do you take me for? Cheek of it!' A look of impudence stole across her face. She hadn't taken offence at my mistake.

I went on the offensive. 'Who's Nora?'

'Nora? Nora Donlan. Poor do.' Her mouth puckered. The same surname as Agnes. Mother or sister?

'Is Nora related to Agnes then?'

'Sister. We don't talk about Nora.'

'What happened to Nora?' I persisted.

She mouthed carefully in a whisper, 'They

141

put her in Kingsfield. Terrible business.'

The penny dropped. And Agnes' flu made some sort of sense.

'Is she here now?' And what would 'now' mean to Lily? Were we still in the war, or before that, during her courtship?

'No, she's not here, she's in the asylum.'

Oh, help. 'Lily, what's the date today?'

'It's August the fifteenth.'

'What year?'

A look of terror descended on her. Her eyes grew wide, her mouth split in a grimace of fear. 'Where's George? I can't find George? What have they done with him? George? George?' She resumed her pacing, beating her fists against her thighs. Gasping for air.

I went in search of a nurse. There were two in the dayroom. The nearest was helping a patient with a drink.

'I've come to visit Mrs Palmer,' I said. 'She's getting quite upset.'

'I'll see to her just as soon as I can.'

'You don't know if her son made it yesterday?'

'Sorry. I wasn't here, I'm on the bank. I cover if they've a lot off sick.'

I went back to say goodbye to Lily. At first I thought she'd left the room. I heard a snuffle from the corner. She was crouched there behind the bed. Hiding.

'Lily, are you all right?'

She looked up and across at me. 'They're taking it all,' she said, 'everything. Thieving from me. They want my soul, you know. And poison. They give me poison.'

'Lily...' I wanted to comfort her but the step I took made her flinch.

'Go away!' she cried. 'Don't you touch me!'

I swallowed, my throat tight. 'Bye-bye, Lily. I'll get the nurse. I'll try and bring Agnes next time.'

She hid her face in the crook of her arm.

In the dayroom the nurse was just wiping the patient's face 'I've not forgotten,' she said cheerily. I waited till she went through to the bedroom.

'Now, Lily...'

I left her to it.

Preoccupied, I reversed out of the parking space. A loud horn blasted. I slammed my foot on the brake, narrowly missing the Audi behind me. The driver glared at me. I shrugged, though my heart was batting and a sheen of sweat had erupted all over my body. I moved back in and let him go past.

Driving home I let my thoughts clatter against each other, not trying to concentrate on anything in particular.

Nora was Agnes' sister and she'd been taken into Kingsfield. Was she still there? Didn't Agnes ever visit? Was guilt the reason for her aversion to going to the hospital? Or had Nora gone long ago? Was it simply memories of bad times that made Kingsfield such a daunting prospect? 'We don't talk about Nora,' Lily had said, 'terrible business.' What had she done? Was Lily referring to the stigma of mental illness or was there something else?

Lily herself was in a bad way: fearful and anxious, and muttering all that stuff about poison – common delusion Mrs Knight had said. Like the stealing. 'They're taking it all,' she'd said. Diane thought I should check her will, must ask Agnes about that. What had Charles found out about her assessment? How were they treating her? Would she stay there?

The road was snarled up with traffic heading up Princess Parkway towards the city. Half the cars sported blue and white scarves. Football. City were playing at home. Diane could watch the match from her bedroom window if she'd wanted to. Her neighbours round the corner were less fortunate; the massive new stand the club had bought not only deprived them of any view but cut off their TV reception for most of the year and rendered their homes impossible to sell. The whole street was seeking compensation.

What was I doing? Saturday afternoon in a traffic jam, shaken up by a visit to a stranger with Alzheimer's. I was here for the money, yes, but the case was becoming absurd. My client was lying to me, and there probably was no case, just an unfortunate set of circumstances.

I felt a surge of anger towards Agnes. I couldn't do a good job without her co-operation. I didn't need excuses and half-truths. By the time I reached my office I'd rehearsed what I wanted to say to Agnes. First, I knew her sister, Nora, had been a patient at Kingsfield. If that meant she couldn't bring herself to visit her friend Lily then so be it. As for me, I was a private investigator not a hospital visitor.

Secondly, as far as I could see, Lily was pretty ill and Agnes would have to work with Charles, next of kin and all that, to press for the best available care.

Third and finally, there was little else I could usefully do other than report back on the analysis of the tablets. Once we'd got the results we'd know if there had been any malpractice by Goulden or Homelea. But for the present Agnes needed to concentrate on making Lily's remaining time as comfortable as possible. The case was practically over.

In the office I intended to jot it all down and work out a provisional bill. It was possible there'd be bad feeling between us and I wanted to make sure Agnes had a report of exactly what work I'd done and my conclusions. Formal and professional in case things got messy.

Best laid plans.

The answerphone was blinking. I realised I'd not taken any messages for a while. I hadn't been in the office since Wednesday, apart from calling in for the negatives with the police, and I hadn't been in a position then to attend to the mundane.

I found pen and pad and pressed play.

Click. 'Sal, it's Rachel. I've lost my diary with your home number in. It is such a drag, I hate losing my diary. So that's why I'm ringing you at work. It's nine o'clock now and I should be in the rest of the morning if you can ring me back. It's about someone I know who's looking for a place to stay. She's just started in our office and she's kipping at her cousin's in Sale at the moment. I thought of you, don't know if you've got anyone yet.

Anyway, give me a ring. Bye.' Click. Beep.

Click. 'It's Jimmy Achebe.' I felt the hairs lift on the nape of my neck, the skin on my face tighten. 'I know I still owe you for the job. I haven't forgotten. Erm ... I'll try and drop it in later this week. Erm ... right then. That's it.' Click. Beep. I pressed pause. My head buzzing with confusion. When had he rung? When had Rachel rung? I was pretty sure I'd cleared my messages on Wednesday. Had the light been blinking when I'd come here with the police on Friday? Tina had been found on Thursday. Surely the last thing a murderer would do would be to ring round settling outstanding bills. Or was that exemplary psychopathic behaviour? No, he must have rung before it all happened. Or maybe the machine had had one of its funny turns and had not shown there were messages waiting on Wednesday.

I pressed play.

Click. 'Sal, Rachel again. Sorry, something's just come up and I've got to go out. It's what ... half-nine nearly and this will probably take me a couple of hours at least so you can try me after twelve, I should be back then. Bye.' Click. Beep.

Click. Beep. Whirr. Someone who didn't like leaving messages. Click. Beep. Whirr.

147

And another.

I reset the machine and cleared my desk.

I'd told Jimmy about Tina on Thursday, the twenty-fourth of February. Exactly a week later she'd died. In the time between had Jimmy been wound up to breaking point, his fury and rage growing till it erupted in such terrible violence, or had he planned her death with ice-cold vengeance?

His message seemed utterly trivial now set against the tragedy he was involved in. I didn't expect I'd ever hear from him again.

I thought back to our last meeting. His hands trembling as he took the photo, the tension in his body, eyes bright with anger. Was there anything I could have said that would have made a difference?

At home I made myself an omelette and ate it while Maddie talked me through her latest set of drawings. I put off ringing Agnes. Tomorrow.

CHAPTER FIFTEEN

Maddie and I got ready for a trip to the park. There was a nip in the air and the clouds were scudding along at a fair old rate so I gathered up gloves, scarves and hats. Maddie got her bike out. I stuffed crisps and apples into my duffel bag. Digger followed me about, desperate to be included. I don't often take him out, there's not a lot of love lost between us and Ray is happy to do all the dog chores, but I'd no excuse for not letting him join our jaunt. First, though, I let him out into the front garden where he could relieve himself shielded from view by thick privet hedges. Since Digger had moved in, the front garden had become his toilet area. We never used it for anything else anyway, too gloomy.

We picked our way round dog dirt all the way to the park, me cursing all the thoughtless dog owners and shouting warnings to Maddie. I let Digger off on the football pitch and he chased demons for all he was worth. Tearing here and there, swerving and changing direction. Maddie pedalled along the path ringing her bell.

We progressed slowly round the park, taking in the dilapidated duck pond with its flooded shores and crumpled railings, the children's play area, the bowling green, the rose garden and the bit we call the wild wood. Here we stopped by a bench and had our picnic, throwing titbits to the squirrels. One was brave enough to take food from our hands. We made it home without an argument.

Sheila was baking. The smell! I was five and begging to lick the bowl, my tongue curling round the metal whisk dripping with sweet yellow goo, nose at table height watching floury hands pat pastry.

'It smells wonderful. Do you do this often?'

'Hardly ever,' she laughed. 'I used to bake twice a week when the boys were little. But not for years. I think it must be a nesting activity.'

'Making the place your own?'

'Yes.' She opened the oven, removed a tray of scones and put in a cake tin. 'It was totally on impulse. I was in the supermarket and I saw the flour and those little bottles of food colouring. I even bought cake tins. Didn't know if you'd have them.'

'Neither do I. If we do they'll be up there

in the cupboard – things we never use.'

Baking. Once all women did it. Lily and Agnes would have grown up knowing how to rustle up a Madeira cake or the recipe for parkin without blinking.

'There was a message for you,' Sheila said. 'The police rang, they left the number, they want you to ring them.'

'Thanks.'

It was Inspector Crawshaw. I dialled and waited. The phone rang on and on. At last it was picked up. I asked switchboard to transfer me to Crawshaw. He was brief and to the point: 'We'd like to have another word. If you're in now I'll send someone round.'

Sergeant Bell turned up twenty minutes later. By then Maddie was engrossed in helping Sheila. I left them in the kitchen and showed the sergeant into the lounge. Would Sheila let Maddie lick the bowl? What about salmonella? It all seemed more complicated these days.

Sergeant Bell flipped open her notebook, checked her watch and noted the time.

'When we last spoke to you, you told us you'd not seen Mr Achebe since Thursday, the twenty-fourth of February,'

'That's right.'

'And he'd not made contact since?' Spoken

slowly, making sure I considered the question carefully.

'Yes, except he'd left a message on my answerphone. I only heard it today, I've not been in the office much. He still owes me some money and he was ringing to say he still intended to pay. It must have been before all this.'

A look of incredulity crossed her face. Then she looked exasperated. 'When was this?'

'I don't know exactly, my machine hasn't got a time announcement. But like I say, it must have been before Thursday, before it all happened. I mean he'd hardly ring me about something so trivial if he'd just killed his wife.' I still couldn't relate the words to an actual death. Couldn't believe Tina was really dead, murdered.

'Do you know what day the message was left?'

'No, not for sure. I could probably find out if you really need to know.'

'We do,' she snapped.

'A friend left a message too. I could ask her, see if she can remember when it was.'

She nodded. The ponytail bounced briskly. 'We'll need the tape.'

'What? Why?'

'I'll take it now.' Bossy. She stood up, pull-

152

ing on gloves.

'Look, I don't know what the big deal is. It's just a message about the bill.'

'The big deal,' she was really rattled now, raising her voice, 'is that James Achebe is suspected of killing his wife. The couple were heard arguing prior to her death.' I'm sure she wouldn't have told me the half of it if she hadn't been so pissed off. 'She was last seen by the postman at nine fifteen that morning; at ten o'clock a neighbour failed to get an answer and notified us. He has no alibi for those forty-five minutes. But,' she glared at me, 'but,' (I had heard her the first time) 'he claims he was at work at the time we estimate the attack took place. No one saw him there until later on. So we've only his word for it. And he claims he made a phone call, rang you.'

'Oh, Jesus.' I felt the blood drop from my face, shock ripple through my wrists and fingers. The answerphone message was Jimmy's alibi.

'What?' Sergeant Bell demanded.

'I've left the machine on. If anyone rings it'll record over it. Oh, shit.'

I ran for my coat, called to Sheila that I'd be out for ten minutes and left with Sergeant Bell. We jogged round the corner. With every step I berated myself. Stupid, sloppy, incompetent.

Grant Dobson was washing the car in their drive. We swapped greetings but I'd no time for being sociable.

I clattered down the stairs, the sergeant at my heels, unlocked my office door.

The answerphone sat on the right side of my desk, its little red message light still and steady. I pressed the off switch. Oh, thank you, thank you, thank you. I pulled out my chair and sank down. Pressed play.

We stood in the gloomy room, breathing harshly, and listened as Rachel's voice burbled on. Then it came. 'It's Jimmy Achebe. I know I still owe you for the job ...' I let it play through. This time I noticed the noises in the background, vans coming and going, the occasional squawk of Tannoy, familiar to me from his previous calls. When Rachel started again I stopped the recording.

'That sounded like his workplace,' I said. 'He's rung me from there a couple of times before.'

She nodded, non-committal.

'You'll contact your friend and find out what day she rang you?'

'Yes.' I tried then and there but all I got was Rachel's answerphone. I reminded her

154

of my home number and asked her to ring me as soon as possible.

'I'll take the tape.'

I ejected it and handed it over.

'We'll be in touch if there's anything else.'

'This might give him an alibi though, might it?'

She zipped up her jacket. 'It's a bit flimsy,' she said. 'All it proves, if we can establish it's Thursday, is that he rang sometime after nine.'

'And before nine thirty.'

She frowned.

I held my hand out for the tape.

'Listen, Rachel says the time again when she rings back. It pinpoints it. Jimmy must have rung in that half-hour.'

I played. Rachel's second message. Sergeant Bell listened. But she didn't give anything away, just nodded when it finished. I gave the tape back to her. She slipped it in a plastic bag, then in her pocket. Pulled on her gloves. And left.

Why hadn't the police asked me directly about any answerphone messages? I wasn't the only sloppy one. If Jimmy had been giving that as an alibi it should have been checked out straightaway. What on earth was the point of all the allusions to whether he'd been in contact when what they had to corroborate was whether a message had been left on my machine that Thursday morning? I felt my cheeks grow warm with rising anger. And because of their beating round the bush the message could so easily have been lost.

I locked up and climbed the stairs. The tape proved that Jimmy hadn't killed Tina. It must be at least half an hour's drive from Levenshulme to Swift Deliveries over the far side of Swinton. Tina had been alive at nine fifteen, dead at ten o'clock and Jimmy had rung me between nine and nine thirty. No way could he have made that call and been in Levenshulme at the crucial time. Jimmy Achebe wasn't a murderer.

But if Jimmy hadn't killed Tina then who the hell had?

CHAPTER SIXTEEN

At home, the cake lay cooling on the side. Maddie stood on a chair at the sink washing up. Totally absorbed.

'She's not shy, is she?' Sheila smiled, tipped her head at Maddie.

'No,' I said. Cranky, opinionated, moody? Yes. Shy? No. 'Wait till the honeymoon's over.'

'You get the worst of it,' she said. 'Mothers do. Do you work with the police much?'

'Oh no, not at all. They wanted to talk to me about a case they're covering. The suspect's an ex-client.'

'Sounds very dramatic.'

'It's not usually,' I said. 'The job is ninety per cent waiting around or looking up forms and checking facts and figures.' The other ten per cent could be particularly hairy, though. I'd been stabbed and shot at on two previous cases where things had turned very nasty.

We were interrupted by the arrival of Ray and Tom. Tea and cakes were devoured and then the demands of domesticity pushed work from my mind.

Saturday had been dominated by the job. Sunday, I restricted myself to a perfunctory phone call to Agnes arranging to see her Monday morning.

Agnes was looking quite chipper when I arrived. She'd made an excellent recovery from the flu. I declined her offer of tea.

I was anxious to get straight down to business.

157

'I went on Saturday,' I began, 'but Lily didn't seem very well at all. She was wandering about when I got there and later she lost track of time. She was talking about the war years and her husband, George. She got – quite distressed too, frightened, claimed that people were stealing from her, trying to poison her. Sounds just like what happened at Homelea.'

Agnes shook her head slowly. 'Oh, Lily,' she muttered.

'What did Charles say? Did you see him?'

She nodded. 'He called in briefly after he'd been to the hospital. Dr Montgomery is doing a full assessment today but he's pretty certain that it is Alzheimer's. He said he hoped he could settle her and she'd be able to move to one of the nursing homes who specialise in it … care of the mentally frail he called it.' She swallowed before carrying on.

'Charles mentioned the business of me being next of kin too, but Dr Montgomery said it would confuse the records and I was welcome to visit at any time. He didn't see any need to complicate matters.'

'So we're going to have to find everything out from Charles?'

'Yes.'

'Agnes, if anything happens to Lily, who

158

inherits her estate?'

She blinked in surprise. 'Charles, there's no one else. Why?'

'It's probably irrelevant but I just wondered if Lily had amended her will recently, made any changes.'

'Not that I know of. I don't understand...' Her face creased deep with confusion.

'Well, I'm trying to consider every possible angle. If there's been any deliberate mal-treatment of Lily we need to think about motives. Who'd want to make her ill, and why? What benefit could there be? If some-one stood to gain financially...'

Agnes stared at me with a look of incredu-lity. It did sound ridiculous. She held up her hand. 'Sal, please don't imagine that I think someone is deliberately mistreating Lily. I only thought there might have been some error of judgement, a mistake, and that people are covering it up. That's why I want you to check the tablets.'

'I've organised that. It'll be a few days before we get the results.'

'Charles was quite shocked at the change in her,' she said. 'I wish there was something I could do.'

'You could visit her for a start.' It came out more sharply than I intended.

'But I...' she was flustered, her hand shook, sought out the brooch on her cardigan, 'I had flu,' she protested.

'And before that it was the chiropodist,' I retorted.

There was an uncomfortable silence. I let it stretch while I curbed my anger. When I spoke I kept my tone deliberately neutral.

'I know about Nora.'

'Nora?'

'Don't, Agnes. Lily told me. Nora, your sister. She ended up in Kingsfield.'

She pressed her hand up to her mouth and struggled to stop the shaking. 'What did she tell you?'

'Not much more than that, really. That Nora was Nora Donlan, she'd been sent to Kingsfield. She gave me the impression it'd been a well-kept secret. No one ever talked about it.'

'I can't, excuse me.' Agnes left the room.

I sat in the quiet and listened to the chirrups from sparrows outside, the occasional puttering sound from the fire. My mouth was dry now. I'd have liked to have got a drink but I didn't dare move and risk intruding on Agnes.

Some time later she came back. Her face was taut and ashen. She clutched a large white hanky but her eyes were dry. She lowered herself into the chair.

'I'm sorry,' she said.

'That's why you've not been to see Lily?'

She nodded in assent.

'Is Nora still there?' I asked.

'No.' She drew a couple of breaths, releasing the air slowly with a shuddering sound. 'No,' she repeated, 'Nora's dead. It was a long time ago.'

'I'm sorry,' I said. The words or perhaps the wobbly note in my own voice served to trigger her tears. Agnes stayed where she was, weeping quietly, almost sedately. She leant forward, buried her face in the hanky. Tears sprang to my own eyes, stinging. I sniffed them back. I went and knelt at her side. Put my arm around her shoulders. She didn't shrug me off. I didn't speak. Agnes wept. At last, taking a couple of deep breaths, she straightened up. I slid my arm away. She turned her head to face me.

'It's more than sixty years ago,' she said, 'sixty years, never mentioned.'

'Do you want to tell me about it?' I offered.

'I'm sorry,' she repeated, 'I can't, I just can't.'

I waited a while before I spoke again. I felt

clumsy, but whatever her emotional state I needed to make my position plain to her. 'Agnes, apart from checking those tablets there's nothing else I can do to help Lily. You and Charles will have to arrange the best care for her. There's no point in my visiting again. She needs friends, people she knows, not me. It's up to you whether you can face it or not. After all, they may move her out into a nursing home.'

'I've been so foolish,' she said, 'so cowardly. Will you come with me tomorrow, please? You're right. It's my place to go. If you could help me, this first time...'

I couldn't say no.

Rachel caught me at home that afternoon.

'Sal, I got back late last night. Weekend in Derbyshire.'

'Not camping?' I was aghast.

'No,' she laughed, 'residential training. Exhausting. You wouldn't believe what goes on and Social Services fork out for it all–'

'Rachel,' I cut in before she launched into a blow-by-blow account, 'when you rang me about the room, what day was it?'

She hummed and hawed a bit. 'Wednesday? No, Thursday.'

'Are you sure?'

'Yes. Wednesday I was in court all day and

162

Friday I went straight off to Derbyshire, it must have been Thursday. Why?'

'Oh, I'd other messages, I needed to work out when they were left.'

'So is it free?'

'What?'

'The room! Honestly, Sal.'

'Sorry, miles away. No, it's gone, we've got someone already.'

'Well, if you hear of anywhere else. This poor woman's getting desperate. Turns out that the cousin is into the Internet in a big way, Worldwide Web, keeps her up till two in the morning enthusing and cruising, or whatever they do.'

I rang the police and got through to Sergeant Bell. I told her it had been Thursday when Jimmy Achebe rang me and left his message. It was an alibi, wasn't it? It was exactly the same time as the attack on Tina. There was no way he could have made it to work all the way over in Swinton in time to ring me if he'd done it. She wouldn't commit herself. Was he still being held? He was. Was there any other evidence to contradict the alibi? She couldn't divulge any information. I felt like throttling her. Why couldn't she bring herself to admit that the tape was pretty

163

watertight proof that Jimmy was innocent? Did the truth not suit the case they'd been building? If she wouldn't tell me anything now I'd make a point of ringing her regularly until she did. If only to remind her that I knew about the alibi and that I expected them to release Jimmy as a result.

I had a cheese salad butty and then cycled to the office supplies place in Didsbury to get a new tape for my answerphone. While I was in the area I called at the cheese shop and stocked up. I was always overwhelmed by the choice but invariably ended up with the same tasty Lancashire, mature Cheddar and a soft Irish blue called Cashell. At the health food shop I bought tinned chickpeas, vegeburger mix, live yoghurt and olives. Everywhere adverts exhorted me to celebrate Mother's Day – with chocolates, flowers, food, teddy bears. There was even a sign attached to the lamppost pushing helicopter rides for Mother's Day, book now! Did they get a rush on like Interflora did?

In the couple of hours left before collecting the children I decided to put some work into the garden. The first weeds were just emerging. I spent time clearing those, digging out myriad small dandelions. Then I shovelled out the compost ready for forking in round the shrubs and in the borders. Over the winter the brick box had got covered with dead wood and brambles. I raked those into a pile for a bonfire. I scraped the bottom of the box clear, all ready for new waste.

We had a large garden which I'd made my own over the years that we'd rented the house. The basics had been there before, lawn, flowerbeds, rockery. To them I'd added a bower-cum-patio next to the house, a suntrap for the long summer afternoons. We'd put a sandpit in for the kids and a climbing frame. And I'd divided off the bottom of the garden with lattices up which I grew clematis, honeysuckle and annual sweet peas. That area got the morning sun.

My plans included a water feature. I'd been keen on the notion of a fountain and pool, but one look at the price of pumps to circulate the water had shifted the scheme from intention to pipe dream. Maybe when my boat came in... I could still go for a pond anyway.

I dug in some of the compost. In the crisp March air it was hard to imagine the scents and colours that summer would bring. By the time I'd done one border my shoulders and back were aching and my time was up. I washed my hands and face, watched the great tits on the bird nuts for a couple of minutes. I'd worked away some of the tension left from dealing with Agnes that morning. And I was thankful that the job, with its erratic nature, at least allowed me time, precious time. For weeding and watching birds feeding and for playing in the soil.

CHAPTER SEVENTEEN

Lily had gone. Agnes and I stood in the room next to the bed she'd occupied. It had been stripped down and made fresh. I looked in the locker. It was empty.

'I'll go and find out what's happening,' I said, sounding more relaxed than I felt. Agnes nodded. She looked bewildered, a tremor shook her lower lip. She'd been tense and silent on the journey to the hospital.

If Lily was dead, how would Agnes bear it? But Lily hadn't been frail, not in that sense, when I'd called on Saturday.

I saw the Irish nurse, whom I'd met before, along the corridor and asked her if we could have a word. She came into the room.

'Do you know what's happened?' I asked

'Mrs Palmer, is it?' She checked.

'Yes.'

'I think she had a fall. They've taken her into the Infirmary. You'd be better talking to Mrs Li. I wasn't on duty.'

Agnes followed me back to the reception area. Mrs Li told us that Lily had fallen early the previous evening. Dr Montgomery had been at the Unit and was able to assess her immediately. He recommended her transfer to the Manchester Royal Infirmary. He suspected that the fall had caused a small bleed to the brain. A scan and X-rays would show whether that was the case and whether there was any need to operate.

'Oh, my goodness,' said Agnes, 'how is she? How did she fall?'

'I really don't know, I wasn't here. We do get a lot of falls,' she tried to reassure us, 'problems with mobility. It was fortunate she was seen so promptly and I'm sure she'll get the very best treatment there. She's gone to the Regional Neurosurgery Unit, Mr Simcock's the consultant. He's very good,' she persisted, 'one of the best neurosurgeons there is anywhere.'

The phone rang and we waited while she answered it.

A woman with ill-matched clothes and

lank grey hair had been hovering nearby, muttering repeatedly to herself. She moved closer, her hands clasped in front of her.

'Did she fall or was she pushed? Answer me that. Humpty Dumpty fell, Baby Bunting fell, atishoo, atishoo, all fall down. They fell. She didn't.'

'Lily,' I said, 'Lily Palmer, did you see what happened? Did she fall?'

The woman shook her head on and on. Did she mean Lily hadn't fallen or that she hadn't seen anything?

'I do not like thee, Doctor Fell, the reason why I cannot tell; But this I know, and know full well, I do not like thee, Doctor Fell. They took her, just like that.' She kissed the air, turned and wandered away. It was impossible to know whether she really had something to tell us or whether she was living in a world of her own.

Mrs Li finished her call. 'I'm sorry, is there anything else?'

I asked her which ward Lily was on.

'I'm not sure. If you find the Neuro-surgical Unit and ask there, they'll tell you.'

It was a fairly direct route up Princess Parkway towards Manchester and the Infirmary. The dual carriageway was always busy; it

168

was one of the main links to the airport and motorways.

'That woman,' I said, 'the other patient, she seemed to think Lily hadn't fallen.'

'Or that she'd been pushed?' Agnes sighed. 'It's one thing after another. First her getting ill, then she's so bad they send her to Kingsfield, now this ... I do hope she's all right.'

'She has fallen before,' I pointed out. 'She can't have been that steady on her feet. It could well be just one of those accidents.'

'I wish there'd been someone...'

I braked sharply to avoid the lorry ahead, whose brake lights were conveniently covered by a lowered tailgate. 'Sorry, go on.'

'It would have helped to talk to someone who'd been there at the time,' she said. 'I didn't get any idea of how serious it might be.'

'I don't think they'd take her in so quickly unless it was urgent. But Mrs Li said they'd do X-rays and scans before they decided if surgery was needed. I suppose they'll know from those how bad she is. It sounded as if she might be all right without any operation.'

'Oh, I hope so. You know, if they are doing a scan,' she said, 'they should also be able to see whether there are changes in the brain, lesions or plaques they call them. There were pictures in one of those books I read. They show up quite clearly on scans, apparently. It could confirm once and for all whether Lily has got Alzheimer's.'

'You're still not convinced about that?'

'No. Not until they prove it to me.'

'But Dr Montgomery, he thinks it's Alzheimer's, doesn't he?'

'Yes. They all do. Charles said they were intending to book Lily in for a scan eventually to look at the extent of the disease but she'd have to go on the waiting list. It's an expensive piece of equipment.'

We reached the Moss Side junction and I turned right past the old Harp Lager place and into Moss Lane East.

'And eighty-five-year-olds aren't exactly a high priority,' she added dryly.

Manchester Royal Infirmary, another red-brick Victorian edifice, sits on the fringe of the university sector just up the road from the Rusholme curry shops. Day and night flocks of students can be seen parading to and from lectures and social events. We parked in the car park at the back and made our way to the main corridor. Murals and mosaics relieved the monotony of the long walk to the ward. The wide corridor bustled with a mixture of staff in various uniforms, visitors in everyday clothes and patients in varying degrees of undress – often swathed in cellular blankets.

At the Neurosurgery Unit we stopped off at the nurses' station. Four nurses were there. They appeared to be discussing papers and one of them was standing and entering notes on a whiteboard. She looked across as we hovered at the door.

'Can I help you?'

'We've come to see Mrs Palmer,' said Agnes. 'She was transferred yesterday evening from Kingsfield.'

'Oh yes, she was admitted last night,' said one of the seated nurses.

'She's gone up, I think,' said another,

'Yes,' said the nurse at the wall, 'she's in pre-op at the moment. It could be quite a while before she's through. There's a waiting room round the corner or you could ring in later.'

'Is there someone we can talk to?' I asked. 'We've only just heard about the fall. We don't know any of the details.'

'I'll see if we can get one of the doctors down to have a word. Would you like to take a seat in the waiting room?'

We went into the lounge, which was empty apart from one woman in a tartan tracksuit watching a quiz show. There was a drinks machine in the corner. I got us each a dubious-looking tea, then went off in search of the toilet.

When I came back Agnes was sitting ramrod straight, looking anxious. 'I've just seen Dr Goulden,' she said.

The tracksuit woman flicked her eyes our way, obviously interested by the tone in Agnes' voice.

'With another man, very tall,' said Agnes.

'Moustache?' checked the woman.

Agnes agreed.

'That was Mr Simcock – he's the brain surgeon. They reckon he's up for a knighthood. Ahead of his time and all that.'

'You know him?' I asked.

'He's looking after my dad. Simcock's done his very best for him. Four operations he's had, counting the one today. Four. Last one took eight hours. Brilliant man. If he's on your case you know you've got the best.' The credits rolled on screen. 'Time for a fag,' she laughed and padded out the room.

'Which way did they go?' I asked Agnes.

'That way – towards the main corridor.'

I had a look round but the two men had

172

gone. Why on earth would a humble GP like Goulden be here with the great brain surgeon? My scant knowledge of how the NHS worked told me that GPs and consultants usually communicated by letter, not in person. I determined to find out a bit more about Simcock and Goulden.

It was almost half an hour before a fresh-faced junior doctor appeared and introduced himself to us. We asked him to tell us what he could about Lily.

'She was admitted after a fall,' he began. 'I think Dr Montgomery suspected there might have been a small bleed, what we call an extradural haematoma. She's in theatre now so they're probably removing a clot and they may need to tie off an artery.'

'But you've not seen her?' Agnes asked.

He hesitated. 'No. Mr Simcock did and he's doing the operation. I'm afraid I don't have her notes here so I can only give you a general idea of what's going on.'

'Can't we see Mr Simcock?' said Agnes.

'I'm afraid he's got a very busy schedule today. If you make an appointment, that would probably be best.'

'How serious is it?' I said. 'Is this ... is it life-threatening?'

'It can be, yes. The fact that she's been seen

quickly and that she's not in coma so they've been able to operate, those are grounds for optimism, but there's no denying it is a critical situation. They could be up in theatre for a while but you're welcome to wait or you could ring the ward for details later.'

Agnes agreed there was no point in waiting.

'Very well, said the doctor, 'goodbye.' He made a point of shaking hands with both of us before he went.

I dropped Agnes off and offered to take her back later – it'd have to be after six as I'd got to pick the children up and feed them. She would ring the hospital to find out when Lily was back from theatre.

I called home for a sandwich and stuck a load in the washing machine. I walked round the corner to work. Where the pavement had flooded, the water had frozen into puddles of ice. The city's low-lying, the land's flat and full of clay, there are countless underwater streams as well as the River Mersey to swell and seep every time it rains. If it's not falling on your head it's creeping up your ankles.

CHAPTER EIGHTEEN

The office was so cold I could see my breath. I switched the convector heater on full and began to defrost. Mused over Lily's moves, from her own home to a residential home, then to the psychiatric hospital, now the Infirmary. Dr Goulden had been very quick to get Lily Palmer out of the community and into the Marion Unit at Kingsfield. There hadn't been any waiting about. Was that unusual? Hoping that Dr Goulden was still out of his surgery I rang his receptionist.

'Hello, it's Jean Brown here from Social Services. I'm just checking on current clinic arrangements between general practitioners and local nursing and residential care homes for the elderly. Now I've got Dr Goulden down for Homelea – does he still run a clinic there?'

'Yes,' she replied, 'and he does Aspen Lodge as well.'

'Oh, yes! Over the page! Thanks for your help.'

Aspen Lodge was in the phone book. This

time I was Monica Saunders researching transfers to the Marion Unit for the Health Commission.

'We're doing an audit now to assess the current attainment targets and the efficiency of the Unit. I need the details of any transfers over the last twelve months.'

'Hang on,' said the woman at the other end, 'I'll have to check the card index.'

'Would you like me to ring back?' I was keen to sound plausible.

'No, it shouldn't take long.' She put the phone down and I could hear the flick of cards and the sound of a radio in the background.

'Hello? We've had four in the last twelve months – since March. Do you want the names?'

'Yes, please,' oh yes, please, 'and dates of birth. Then I can cross-check with our records.'

'Mrs Rose Mary Connelly – fourth of the ninth, 1914. Miss Margaret Anne Underwood – eleventh of the sixth, 1905. Mr Philip Braithwaite – sixteenth of the first, 1903, and Mrs Winifred Saltzer – twenty-third of the tenth, 1916.'

'And have they remained at Kingsfield?'

'You'd have to check with the hospital.

176

None of them came back here.'

'Thank you.'

Would Homelea be as forthcoming? Not if I got the icy Mrs Knight. I steeled myself. I got her. I did my spiel and waited.

'Where did you say you were from?'

'Resources, research, monitoring and management – we come under the Health Commission administration. We were only established this year so you may not have heard of us before. I can leave my number if you'd prefer to ring us back with the inform-ation.'

'Yes.'

I sat watching the phone repeating my alias over and nover to myself. I let it trill twice before picking it up. 'Resources, re-search, Monica Saunders speaking.'

'Sorry,' mumbled a voice at the other end, 'wrong number.'

'Who is it?' I yelped.

'Is that Sal?'

'Yes.'

'It's Diane. What are you playing at?'

'Work. Look, can I ring you back? I'm waiting for a call.'

'Oh, go on then.'

As soon as I replaced the handset it went again. I picked it up and said my bit.

'It's Homelea here,' said Mrs Knight. 'We've had two transfers to Kingsfield this year.'

'Can I check the names and dates of birth with you? I've only got a Mrs Palmer listed and that was very recent.'

'The other was Mr Ernest Theakston.'

'Now, we've not got him down for some reason. I'll have to check the records again. What's the date of birth?'

'Second of the twelfth, 1922.'

'Thank you for your help. Goodbye.'

Six patients transferred to Kingsfield in the last year, from just two homes. Homes with the same GP. And the Marion Unit wouldn't have a large number of beds. Apart from Saltzer, they were all common names, not that easy to track down. I checked the phone book. There was a Saltzer in Gorton and one in Chorlton. I tried the Gorton number first, they'd never heard of Winifred. But the man in Chorlton had. He was her widower.

'She passed away in October,' he said. 'Who is this?' I didn't want to lie but I couldn't tell him the bald truth.

'My name's Palmer, Sal Palmer. My great-aunt has gone into Kingsfield – she was at Aspen Lodge for a while. My grandmother is beside herself with worry. I thought it might

178

help if I talked to relatives of other patients – then I could tell Grandma what people thought of the care there. She's talking about going private, you see, but we really can't afford it.'

He didn't ask how I'd got his number or anything. 'Well, we'd no problem with the set-up there. They did all they could, lovely staff. But ... I don't know what happened to Winnie, it's not going to be that reassuring for your grandmother, is it? She had Alzheimer's, you see, and there's no treatment yet. Mr Simcock, he's the neurosurgeon at the Infirmary, he was very good as well. She went there for a scan, you know; they can see exactly what's going on. But there was nothing they could do for her really. It's a terrible thing.'

'I am sorry. Had she been at Aspen Lodge for a long time?'

'Three years. I couldn't manage her at home. I've angina myself and she was wandering a lot. She settled in all right. It was a lovely home – well, you'll know yourself. Then she started getting very agitated, last summer. She became very confused, she wouldn't eat. She didn't know who I was any more, couldn't remember her own name from one minute to the next. Dr Goulden thought she'd be better off at the Marion Unit. Like I said, they really did their best for her. She was in there just two months before she died.'

I thanked him for talking to me.

There were some similarities in the path that both Winifred Saltzer and Lily Palmer had taken, although from the sound of it Winifred had been ill for several years before going to Kingsfield – nothing like the sudden deterioration that Lily had undergone.

Mr Saltzer's willingness to help prompted me to try contacting relatives of some of the other patients. I thumbed the phone book and started by calling the names listed as living in South Manchester. I spent an intensive hour on the phone. My luck held. It was one of those days when everyone was in and happy to talk. I was flying. Some days I get nothing but answerphones or people being cagey, obstructive, stroppy.

I've always wondered what determines the pattern – me or them.

I crowed as I put down the phone after the last call. Did a little dance round the office. I'd found everyone bar Ernest Theakston.

The information I'd assembled didn't tell me anything earth-shattering but there were some interesting facts.

180

Of the six patients transferred by Goulden to the Marion Unit at Kingsfield three suffered a slow decline and were moved there not long before the disease killed them. Ernest Theakston was an unknown and the other two people Lily Palmer and Philip Braithwaite – had become ill more rapidly. Mr Braithwaite had not only had dementia but a scan had revealed a brain tumour. A biopsy had been done at the MRI but Mr Simcock felt it was too late to operate.

'He was on tablets,' his daughter had said, 'to try and calm him down but there wasn't anything else they could do for him.' As it was, the tumour hadn't killed Mr Braithwaite: he'd caught flu while in hospital and died there.

Was Ernest Theakston dead too? It wouldn't be unexpected. These were elderly, often frail patients, so ill that they could no longer be nursed at Aspen Lodge or Homelea.

Time for school pick-up. I still needed to ring Diane back, I wanted to give Moira a nudge over the tablets and I hadn't done anything yet to find out more about any links between Goulden and Simcock. I didn't get a chance to do anything until after six o'clock. The

181

kids were both in needy mode. Tom had developed a cold, which gave him a pair of permanent green nose-candles and an uncharacteristic tendency to whine. Maddie couldn't bear the diversion of attention and promptly came up with tummy ache and a sore ear. I dispensed drinks and toast and honey and proceeded to read stories to them – the only activity they'd both go along with.

At half-five we had beans on toast and when Ray came in I asked him to take over. He loaded Snow White into the video.

I spoke to Diane first, arranging to meet up later in the week. There was no answer from Moira's. I rang the surgery; she'd appointments booked up until seven o'clock.

Agnes had got through to the hospital, though, and Lily was back on the ward. We could visit any time before eight o'clock but she'd still be asleep.

'I could get a taxi,' Agnes offered.

'No, you're fine,' I replied. 'Are you ready now?'

I explained to Ray and the children that I needed to pop out. Maddie burst into tears and clung to my leg.

'But I don't want you to go. I want you to put me to bed.' She wasn't going to listen to logic. I promised to come and check on her

182

as soon as I got back. Together Ray and I prised her off.

'Mummee,' she wailed, 'Mummee, don't go, please, Mummee.'

My stomach curled round on itself. 'I'll be as quick as I can.' I fled.

I was an awful mother. How could I do this to my child? And how could she make me feel so bloody awful?

CHAPTER NINETEEN

Agnes and I made the same long trek to the ward where Lily was. Clusters of visitors gathered round the beds. The curtains were drawn around Lily's. She was asleep and her head was bandaged.

We pulled up chairs on either side of the bed. Agnes took Lily's hand in her own. I said I'd go see if there was anyone about we could talk to, left them to it.

There was a new shift of nurses on duty. When I enquired about Lily one of them checked the board. 'Post-op. She's had the surgery. She'll probably sleep through till the morning. We'll be checking on her

183

throughout the night.'

'Do you know how it went?' I asked.

'Not in detail,' she smiled, 'but she's resting now and everything seems to be going as we'd expect. It'll be several days before we can be sure. They'll do more scans to check and so on but she seems to be doing very well so far.'

I reported back to Agnes. Lily lay very still. Only a slight but regular movement in her throat showed us she was breathing.

'I've been finding out a bit about Dr Goulden's caseload,' I said. Agnes was listening attentively. 'He's referred six patients to Kingsfield in the last twelve months. I don't know how many beds there are but the place is meant to serve the whole of South Manchester, and those six are from just one GP, just two homes.'

'Were any of them like Lily? Did any of them seem all right until they went into the home?'

'Maybe one, a bloke called Philip Braithwaite. He seemed to go downhill quickly, then they found a tumour, they did a biopsy but he got flu and died while he was here.'

'So it could have been the tumour that complicated things,' she mused. 'And the others?'

'Classic symptoms, nothing unusual, came here for scans, ended up in Kingsfield.'

We were interrupted by the nurse I'd spoken to earlier. She wanted to check Lily's pulse and temperature.

Agnes asked how long Lily would be in hospital and whether she could tell us if the scans they had done had told them anything about her Alzheimer's.

'I'm sorry,' she made notes on the chart and clipped it back on the bed, 'I don't know. You need to speak to Mr Simcock about that.'

At eight o'clock we left, along with the last of the other visitors, and I drove Agnes home. She wanted to speak to Charles and I was keen to find out what he knew. I followed her through to her back room where the phone was. It was bitterly cold and we both kept our coats on. The room was much more lived in than her lounge and still sported an old-fashioned creel suspended from the ceiling where clothes could be hung to dry. Edges of green lino showed around the large Indian rug that covered most of the floor. The wallpaper was some faded leaf design and here and there paintings and old photos hung. She lit the gas fire and left it on full. She found and dialled the number.

'Charles? It's Agnes Donlan here. I've just been to see your mother. Have you spoken to the hospital today? That's right, bleeding in the brain and the operation is to clear it up. Was it Mr Simcock you spoke to? Yes, and what did he say? Good, and what about the Alzheimer's? Really? Oh dear. When did they tell you about the fall? Well, I wish you'd let me know. I had no idea until I went to see her at the Marion Unit and she'd gone. It was an awful shock... Yes, I realise that but I really wouldn't have minded. You can ring me at any time, I want you to... Pardon? Consent, what for? Oh, I see. Well, I suppose they have to check... She was fast asleep but the nurse said she was doing as well as could be expected. Are you planning to come up? I see.'

Agnes wasn't best pleased by his answer. She looked over at me and raised her eyes to heaven. 'Well, please let me know what you find out,' Agnes was saying. 'It's hard for me to get any decent information and I would like to be kept informed. I'll be going to see her again tomorrow.' She said her goodbyes and put the phone down.

She sighed with exasperation. 'They rang him about the fall as soon as she was admitted but he didn't like to ring me late at night.

Honestly!' She shook her head impatiently. 'When I've made it plain all along that I want to be told what's happening. I'm the only friend she has left.' She took a deliberate breath. 'He says Mr Simcock said the operation had gone very well. She isn't out of the woods yet but he said they were hopeful. But the scans confirmed she has Alzheimer's and he said it was pretty advanced.' She sighed again, massaged her temples with her fingers. She looked drained.

'He's planning to come up at the weekend and keep in touch with the hospital by phone.'

'What was that about consent?'

'Oh,' she pulled a face, 'they had to make sure Charles knew that Lily was an organ donor and see if he had any objections to her wishes.'

'You're joking!'

'No, a precaution apparently, but as the doctor pointed out to him Lily is getting on in years and it's better to think about it now than at the time of death. Lily always said she wanted to help others if she could. She gave blood for years.' She stood up. 'It's so frustrating having to hear everything second-hand from Charles, when he's miles away.' She tutted. 'Would you like some tea?'

'No, I'd better be getting back. I'd like to know why Goulden was at the hospital with Mr Simcock today. I could do a bit of digging.'

'Yes,' said Agnes, 'I'd like you to. And the tablets?'

'I'll try and talk to my friend again – she might be able to hurry things up a bit.'

The car had iced up again and the pavement glittered dangerously with black ice. I scraped the screen and turned on the fan. My shoulder ached with fatigue, I rolled it around, stretched my neck, leant my head back against the head rest. It was slightly more comfortable but I couldn't see as much of the road surface as I needed to. I hunched forward over the wheel and drove slowly home.

Maddie was asleep, lying flat on her back, her arms flung above her head. I sat there for a few minutes gazing at her. In the other bed Tom snuffled with his cold, coughed now and then, but Maddie slept on undisturbed.

'Moira. It's Sal. Any news on those tablets?'

'No. But I didn't put them in as urgent so they wouldn't hurry – and they'd certainly not have touched them over the weekend. Other jobs will get done first. I told you it'd be a few days.'

'I know. Just impatient. What do you know about the neurosurgeon Simcock?'

'He's famous – brilliant reputation. Keeps threatening to leave and work overseas. Reckons the profession's being bled dry. He's had a lot of stuff in the Lancet – keen on the new technology: lasers, biogenetics too, if I remember right. Why do you ask?'

'He's treating the woman whose case I'm working on.'

'The one with the tablets?'

'Yes. She's had a fall and a haemorrhage in the brain. They've had to do an operation. What about Dr Montgomery, up at Kingsfield, at the Marion Unit?'

'Can't stand him. This is all confidential I hope?'

'Of course.'

'Probably competent in his own way but he's obsessed with drugs. Chemical answer to everything. Sort who gives Prozac out like Smarties. Pharmaceutical companies love him. I've not had a lot of direct contact but you get to hear about people. Has he been treating this woman too?'

'Yes. She went from Homelea to Kingsfield and now with this fall, she's gone to the MRI.'

'Well, they reckon Simcock's the best there is. If there's anything to be done surgically he's your man.'

'How many psycho-geriatric beds are there for South Manchester?'

'Is this a trick question?'

I laughed. 'No. I think someone might be getting more then their fair share.'

'I can't tell you offhand. Fifty or so I think.'

'Could you check for me?'

'Yes.'

'And they're all based at the Marion Unit?'

'That's right.'

'Thanks. And if there's anything you can do to speed up the lab results on the tablets...'

'I'll see what they say. Don't bank on it. Later.' She signed off in the same old way.

I scoured the evening paper looking for anything about the Achebe case. There was nothing in. Was Jimmy still being held in spite of his alibi? How could they do that? The only way he could have killed Tina and also phoned me from work was if they'd been mistaken about the time of death, but the neighbour's testimony had sounded very precise. Perhaps they had released him but not in time for the paper to get hold of the story. Presumably they'd also interviewed the man I'd seen meet Tina at the hotel, if they could trace him. After all, if Jimmy was innocent he must be the next most likely suspect.

The only way I could get warm was to run a hot bath and lie there till the steam cleared. There was a hot, prickly feeling in the back of my throat. I made some tea with honey and lemon and sipped it while reading in bed. I woke deep in the night, shivering with cold, no covers on me at all. Maddie had crept in with me and snaffled them all. I was too tired to try moving her so I redistributed the duvet, rearranged her elbows and sank back to sleep.

Maddie woke at half-past six as usual, waking me too. My tongue had dried out and swollen up like a huge prune. I gulped down some water, provided Maddie with cereal, milk and television and crawled back to bed. I woke again to Ray calling me. It was time to get them ready for school. He was back on the conversion job so I couldn't ask him to do it. My cold had come on with a vengeance, everything felt muffled, my head was swimming and the walk to school was exhausting.

I didn't feel up to much but nevertheless set off for the library. In the research section I flipped through back copies of the Lancet

191

till I found two articles by Matthew Simcock. One was about current developments in the understanding of Alzheimer's, known and suspected changes in the physical tissues of the brain. The other article was a plea for more funding for research into biogenetics and neurology. I didn't understand much of either, they certainly weren't written for the layperson.

On the way to the office I mused over the connection between the doctors: Goulden the GP, Montgomery the psycho-geriatrician and Matthew Simcock the neurosurgeon. Goulden and Montgomery dealt with Lily because they specialised in geriatric care. Simcock was only brought in when it seemed that surgery might help, although judging by the articles he certainly had an interest in senile dementia for which there was no effective treatment, surgical or otherwise.

I rooted around for any other connections – they all worked in Manchester? My brain was too soggy to concentrate. I switched track. Suppose Dr Goulden was referring an unusually high number of patients through to Kingsfield – to what possible advantage? Would he or the consultant get some sort of piece-work bonus? It couldn't work like that because the number of beds at the Marion Unit was limited and in great demand. Montgomery would hardly thank him for increasing the pressure on resources. It couldn't be anything to do with legacies and inheritance either. Wills had to be drawn up while people were 'of sound mind', not altered while under the care of a psychiatrist. I finally admitted to myself that I couldn't think of a single dodgy reason why Goulden might be sending people on to Kingsfield.

The answerphone light blinked. Moira had left me a message. 'Sal, sixty beds at Kingsfield. Thirty-five continuing care, the rest acute, that includes assessment beds.'

It was bigger than I'd guessed, but even so, Gouliden's patients had taken a tenth of the available beds in one year. On the other hand, if they hadn't stayed long perhaps it wasn't that unusual. Then think of all the other GPs, all the other old people's homes – there was one of them on every corner around Withington and Didsbury. The big red-brick villas that no one could afford to buy were ideal for conversion and there was no shortage of people looking for residential care. A lot of the homes had people with Alzheimer's and continued to care for them.

Was I making a mountain out of a molehill? Were six transfers in a year over the top, par for the course, or just a statistical blip?

I made a strong coffee and sat at my desk, feet up. I'd no motive, no connection. Why had my suspicions been aroused? The six referrals, the chance sighting of Goulden and Simcock together and the fuss around the tablets, Goulden's tantrum and Mrs Knight's lies. Innocent explanations could probably be found for any of those.

Connections. I sipped my coffee, it had no taste; catarrh had joined my list of symptoms... I could always try Harry. He was an old friend whose career in journalism and love for information had led him into the world of databases, data retrieval and the supply of information. He was now a popular contact for investigative reporters and researchers. He specialised in the business and commercial sectors and could find out more or less anything factual about people, companies, deals and contracts. It was a long shot – I didn't know whether his range covered the world of medicine but I'd no other ideas pending.

I got through straight away.

'How's it going with Sheila?'

'Fine. I think she likes it here. She's nice.'

'She was over the moon when you offered her it, she rang us later. That place she was before – horrendous. So what can I do for you?'

I explained that I was looking for anything, that might link any of the names Dr Kenneth Goulden, Mr Matthew Simcock and Dr Douglas Montgomery together. I already knew they were all in medicine and all worked in Manchester. 'There's probably nothing,' I warned him, 'but I'm short on ideas.'

'It'll be a joy,' he said. 'I'm up to my eyeballs in share dealings in the major utilities so this'll be a doddle. You sound terrible,' he commented.

'I feel terrible, a cold.'

'Get to bed then,' he said. 'I'll talk to you later.'

I took his advice. Before I left I tried to get hold of Sergeant Bell; she was busy. They asked if I wanted to leave a message.

'Tell her it's Sal Kilkenny. I'm ringing to see if there's any news about Jimmy Achebe.'

They assured me that Sergeant Bell would get the message as soon as she was available.

I stuck my answerphone on, locked up the office and went home. Before getting into bed I rang Agnes and explained I was poorly and wouldn't be up to taking her to see Lily. She was understanding and said she could easily get a taxi.

I set my alarm for three o'clock, drank half a pint of orange juice, swallowed two aspirin and snuggled under the duvet.

The rest of the day passed. About all you could say for it really. I went through the motions, muffled in cold, and escaped to an early bed as soon as possible. I woke once, rearing up from the dream where I was being suffocated. Someone was squashing my nose. At the time I put it down to having a blocked-up nose. Now, looking back, I wonder whether it was intuition.

CHAPTER TWENTY

The weather had warmed up again and there were even patches of fresh blue sky here and there. I didn't particularly welcome the change; my temperature was all over the place, sweaty one minute, chilled the next. To my teary eyes the bright sky was painful to look at. My cold was now in full spate, swallowing no longer hurt but breathing was difficult. I was in a diving bell, sound echoed and distorted and all the colours were too vivid. With pockets stuffed full of hankies I walked Maddie and Tom to school. I wondered about another day in bed but it seemed excessive for a cold, lousy though I felt. I compromised, telling myself I'd see how I was by lunchtime.

At the office I opened my heap of junk mail. I was exhorted to borrow money, install a new security system, send away for a free gift (matching towels or handy holdall), order two pizzas for the price of one and have my carpets cleaned half-price. I binned the lot. Even resisting the temptation to use the scratch card that would reveal whether I'd won £10, £50 or £10,000. Fat chance.

There were no messages on my answerphone. I jotted down notes on the Lily Palmer case and recorded visits I'd made, entering time and mileage on separate sheets. I sat and pondered for a while, letting the coincidences and questions nibble away at me.

The small basement window was filthy. It occurred to me that I could probably double the amount of light in the place if I cleaned it and took down the broken blind. All the Dobsons were out but I knew they wouldn't mind if I borrowed a bit of window cleaner and a cloth. They had a cupboard under the sink with cleaning stuff in. I found what I wanted and proceeded back downstairs. I stood on my chair and pulled at the roller blind, the whole thing came away easily. I dropped it on the floor, gave the spiders time to run for cover, then squirted the glass. The grime came off in satisfying swathes but the outside needed doing too.

I went upstairs and outside, knelt down by the window and stretched across the gap to swipe away the webs strewn with debris, fragments of curled leaf, scraps of paper and seeds. I wiped the dust and rain marks from the pane. By then I was running with sweat and trembling with exhaustion.

I put the cleaning stuff back, washed my hands and sat down to rest. I was hungry. Feed a cold and starve a fever. I felt as though I'd got both but there was no contest, appetite won out. I couldn't taste the sandwich I made myself back home but it stopped the growling in my belly. I napped on the sofa for an hour and felt human once more.

I called Sergeant Bell again. She was still busy. I wasn't content to leave yet another message. I asked whether I could speak to Inspector Crawshaw. He was busy. I could leave a message.

'Is there anyone who can give me some information?'

'Concerning?'

'Jimmy Achebe. Is he still in custody? Have any charges been brought?'

'You could try the Press Office.' He gave me the number. It was busy.

Instead, I called Agnes to find out the latest. Lily had not been very well when she'd visited. She'd had a high temperature that they were concerned about and they suspected an infection. She was asleep all the time that Agnes was there. Agnes was worried. 'At our age this sort of thing can be so much harder to shake off.'

'I am sorry. Any news from Charles?'

'Yes. He's spoken to Mr Simcock again. There's no reason to suspect there's any connection between the operation and the infection. Apparently just being in hospital increases the risk. He said they'll be concentrating on trying to fight that off using antibiotics. But even if she gets over all this she's never going to be well. You know, the scan showed substantial changes in her brain.' I could hear the desolation in her voice. She cleared her throat. 'There's very little they can do now. All we can expect is a steady decline.'

'Will she go back to Kingsfield?'

'I'm not sure. Charles got the impression they were thinking of one of the nursing homes where they specialise in caring for patients with Alzheimer's. I've been thinking about it a lot. I suppose I've got the proof I wanted about Lily's condition: they've defin-ite physical evidence of what's wrong. Now I need to accept it. It's not going to go away. I just hope she can shake off this infection.'

'Do you want to see her tonight? I could give you a lift.'

'You don't sound very well,' she said doubtfully.

'No, I'm all right. Just this cold. I'll come about six.'

'Thank you. Oh, by the way, it doesn't seem so important any more but did you hear anything more about the tablets?'

'No. I've asked my friend to chivvy the lab along. She's doing me a favour so I can't really push her any more than I have done. I'm also trying to find out if there's any con-nection between Goulden and Simcock but I've not got anything yet. I'm waiting to hear.'

I did hear. Just after I got back from school, Harry rang. 'Hi! I've left a message on your answerphone too,' he began.

'Any luck?' I didn't expect anything.

'Bingo!'

'What?' I was astonished.

'You got a fax yet?'

'No.'

'A pen?'

'Yes, Harry, I have a pen. Poised. Go on.'

'OK. Simcock and Montgomery are both directors of Malden Medical Supplies.'

My scalp prickled.

'They're a company based in Cheshire, Northwich, and they supply anything and everything – rubber gloves, gas cylinders, disposable sheets, bandages, the lot. They deal with nursing homes, hospitals, that sort of thing. It's a lucrative little concern, accounts for the last year on record show a turnover of two million and very healthy profits.'

'Hang on, let me get this all down.' I scribbled furiously. 'Right.'

'That was up fifty per cent on the previous year. They came in just at the right time, when all the privatisation was kicking in and the fact that the clients can get all their stuff from the same supplier probably gave them the edge over the competition.'

'So, they'll be making quite a bit from it?' I said.

'Oh, yeah. Depends how much they're ploughing back in but they're doing very nicely thank you.'

'Nothing illegal?'

'Well, the law's very woolly around some of this, but everything I've told you so far is public knowledge somewhere or other. Difference is it'd take you weeks going via other agencies, hard copies. Using the computer makes it that much quicker...'

'Harry! I didn't mean you. I meant them – anything fishy about their operation?'

'Oh, no. Nothing glaring anyway.'

'And Goulden's not a director?'

'Ah-ha! No. But listen to this. There's a Mrs A. L. Goulden, BPharm, MRPharmS, who's actually Managing Director.'

'His wife.'

'There's more – her maiden name was Montgomery, Angela Leonie Montgomery, sister to Douglas Vernon Montgomery.'

'Yes!' The connections were there. They all had some involvement in Malden Medical Supplies, and Montgomery and Goulden are brothers-in-law.

'Anything else you want? Creditworthiness, mortgage details, hire purchase agreements?'

'Spare me.'

'Seriously, Sal, you ought to think about getting a system. The amount of stuff you'd have there at your fingertips.'

Oh yeah, and the amount of time it'd take me to access it. 'I can't even afford a fax at the moment, Harry.'

'Tax deductible.'

'I don't pay enough blinking tax to deduct it. Besides, it's money up front which I can't manage.'

'Or credit.'

'I wouldn't dare.'

'Shame. Plenty of your lot are in there already, you know.'

'Yeah, well, lucky I got you, isn't it?'

'Why keep a dog and bark yourself?'

I laughed. 'Something like that. Besides, you're an expert. You'll let me know if it gets too much?'

'Go on. But promise me...'

'What?'

'If there's a story...'

'I thought you'd given up on journalism.'

'Oh, I still need a nice juicy scandal now and again. One that I write up instead of seeing it mangled by the other hacks.'

'You'll be the first to know. But don't hold your breath.'

So there were plenty of legitimate reasons for Goulden and Simcock to meet at the hospital, a word about business if not a conscientious visit from the GP concerned about his elderly patient.

But I wasn't thinking about legitimate reasons. I was more interested in the other sort.

By quarter to six I was regretting my offer to take Agnes to the hospital but I didn't want to let her down at the last minute. Ray still wasn't in from work so I resorted to going up and asking Sheila if she'd keep an eye on the children till he got back. She was happy to. I braced myself for another tantrum from Maddie but she didn't turn a hair when I explained what was happening. I was the only one who was uncomfortable with the situation because I felt I was imposing on Sheila.

On our journey to the Infirmary I told Agnes about the business and family links between the three doctors. 'Mr Simcock is on the board of directors there and Mrs Goulden is the Managing Director so that could be one reason why we saw Dr Goulden at the hospital – he's got business connections with Simcock.'

Silence. 'Agnes?'

'Let me get this right. Mr Simcock is on the board of the company?'

'Yes.'

'And Dr Montgomery?'

'Yes. And what's more, Mrs Goulden, who

204

works there, is actually the sister of Dr Montgomery too. It's very incestuous.'

'I don't like it,' she said sharply.

'It stinks,' I agreed, 'and there are too many coincidences flying around. All these people have been involved in Lily's treatment – is that just because it's a specialised area? Is it just nepotism, the old boy network, or is there something else going on?' I was speculating aloud.

Agnes shook her head.

'You'd think one well-paid job would satisfy,' she remarked, 'with all this unemployment.'

'It might be greedy but it's not illegal,' I pointed out. 'Besides, they're directors of the business – they employ people to work there.'

'And money makes money. Always has done. What about them?' She pointed towards a cluster of youths who were gathered outside a local off-licence. 'Nothing, no hope. Even in the thirties there was hope, the belief that things could change. Now ... all this talk about moral standards and the fabric of society. A return to Victorian values. Huh,' she snorted, 'Victorian values were savage, smothered in hypocrisy.'

I was fazed at her outburst and I'd no idea what had set her off. I said nothing. We arrived at the hospital.

The curtains were still drawn round Lily's bed and no sooner had we sat down at her bedside than a junior doctor arrived. She introduced herself and explained that they were using intravenous antibiotics to try to fight the infection that had raised Lily's temperature. The saline drip was to prevent dehydration.

'Has she been awake?' asked Agnes.

'She's been sleeping. That's no bad thing, rest can help a great deal.'

'Is she going to be all right?'

The doctor didn't give her a straight answer, she probably couldn't. 'If we can get her over the infection there's no reason why she shouldn't make a complete recovery from the haematoma.' She left.

Agnes slid her hand under Lily's. The face on the pillow was peaceful enough but her breath was harsh and ragged, painful to listen to.

'I'll wait in the lounge for a bit,' I offered. 'Don't want to give her this cold on top of everything else.'

Half an hour later I returned. I was ready to go. The heat on the ward was making me sweat, my head had started pounding and I was beginning to feel unsteady, slightly dizzy.

As I slipped behind Agnes and touched her shoulder, Lily woke. She stared at Agnes, then blinked slowly.

'Lily. Lily, it's Agnes. You've not been well, you're in the MRI.' Lily blinked. I wondered how much she could see without her glasses on.

'Olive,' it was a hoarse whisper, 'my Olive.'

'Oh, Lily.' Agnes stroked her hand.

Lily closed her eyes again and soon the noisy, dragging breath returned. Persistent but irregular. Gently Agnes released her friend's hand.

'Olive was her daughter,' she said. 'She died a week after her third birthday. Milk sickness, TB.'

She stood up. We made our way slowly and in silence past the bright murals down the long corridor to the exit.

CHAPTER TWENTY-ONE

'MAN CHARGED IN ACHEBE SLAY-ING. HUSBAND RELEASED,' brayed the evening paper. Front-page news. Complete with one of the shots I'd taken of the man

I'd seen at the hotel with Tina Achebe.

I sank into the chair, my coat still on, and scanned the text. He was named as Bill Sherwin, forty-two, a local businessman. There was nothing about why he might have murdered Tina, though much was made of the fact that they were both married. A police spokesman was quoted as saying forensic reports were still being prepared. No further details could be released at present. The paper rehashed details of Tina's death, included quotes from neighbours and family about their response to both Jimmy's release and Sherwin's arrest, and showed a photo of the terraced house complete with police tape across the gate.

The police were also eager to hear from anyone who had been in that area of Levenshulme that day, who might have seen anything, perhaps without realising it, that could help build up a picture of the events that morning. It was clear that Bill Sherwin had not confessed to the killing and that they were still building the case against him.

I felt a wave of relief that Jimmy was innocent, and by implication that the murder of Tina Achebe had not been the result of my revelations. Unless ... a fresh grub of guilty worry hatched as I wondered whether

Sherwin had killed Tina because of the chain of events I'd set in motion: I told Jimmy, Jimmy confronted Tina, Tina told Sherwin...

Oh stop it, I admonished myself. Jimmy was free. And what horror had he been through these past days? Losing Tina, brutally murdered – that was enough to destroy anyone. But then to be accused of that murder, to be suspected, held, questioned. The rage he must have felt, the agony of it.

I made myself a strong hot toddy – whisky, water, lemon and honey – and watched the television news, waiting for the regional slot that followed. There was a report on Jimmy's release with a brief film clip of him getting into an unmarked car, and shots of the house in Levenshulme and of Manchester Crown Court.

I retreated to bed. I looked in on the children on the way up. We don't expect to outlive our children but Tina Achebe had died before her time. And Lily Palmer, she had lost her three-year-old daughter. How had she borne it? Had it been any more bearable back in the days when so many children died in infancy? I didn't think so, although perhaps the rituals were there then, the means to acknowledge and mark the deaths of young ones. A child had died in Maddie's class the previous year, a road accident. The whole neighbourhood had reeled with the shock. He had older brothers at the school too. They'd held a special assembly for him, Maddie had been full of it. I hadn't known the family, I hadn't felt I had any right to speak with the mother, not even to offer condolences. I'd bought a bunch of flowers instead and left them in the pile of cellophane bundles by the lamppost beside the road where the accident had happened.

I pulled the covers over Tom and picked up the bath towels from the floor. Once in my own bed I lost myself in the Louisiana swamplands with James Lee Burke as I sipped the pungent brew. The dog down the road was barking loud enough to waken the dead. I fantasised half a dozen ways to silence it and lulled myself to sleep.

I couldn't put off a supermarket trip any longer. We were out of all the basics. After the school run I drove round there and stocked up. No matter how frugally I intended to shop I always ended up with items that weren't on the list. I had once tried going to one of the new super-cheap outlets but there were so many things they didn't sell that I'd had to do another shop the following day and spent just as much in the long run.

With the cupboards and fridge full I felt a small glow of satisfaction and as I'd used my credit card to pay I didn't need to worry about the bill until next month.

I pottered through the afternoon. Ray had done a load of washing. I transferred it to the dryer. I tidied and cleaned the lounge, hoovered round. My cold was getting better but was still bad enough to slow me down. My energy was low. I sat in the kitchen with a cuppa. I really ought to think about winding up the case for Agnes. It all seemed to be petering out.

The phone rang.

'Sal? Moira. Where the hell did you get those tablets?'

'I told you, from a client. This GP, Goulden, had prescribed them for the woman in the rest home, the one we thought might have acute confusion. Her friend found them in her things. Is there something the matter?'

'Should think she did have bloody confusion.'

'Why?'

'For a start they're four times the marked dosage. Each tab's got a hundred milligrams of thioridazine in. She'd be getting two

211

hundred milligrams a day, not fifty. Were they giving her anything else?'

I thought back to the conversation at Dr Goulden's surgery. 'She got nitrazepam at night sometimes – to help her sleep.'

Moira snorted. 'Classic. Adverse reaction. She's getting massive doses of thioridazine – that's enough in itself to make her disoriented and confused, induce panic attacks, breathing difficulties alternating with drowsiness – then they're topping her up with nitrazepam. That's making her even worse. She'll be staggering around, peeing the bed, maybe even hallucinating, showing signs of psychosis. Enough to make anyone demented.'

They give me poison, that's what Lily had said. They want my soul.

'He said he'd look again at the dosage, Dr Goulden, when we talked to him. He said sometimes it took a while to get the balance right.'

'Sal, all they needed to do was stop the medication and the symptoms would have stopped. It's one of the first things that should be considered in cases like this but some GPs are that bloody cocksure. What's he called? Goulden?'

'Yes.'

'Don't know him. Where's he based?'

'Didsbury.'

'The poor bloody woman probably hasn't got Alzheimer's at all.'

'No, she has. They've just done a scan at the MRI and she's got the lesions apparently.'

'Well, I don't know where this Goulden chap had the script prepared but it must be some Mickey Mouse set-up. Four times the stated dosage. I ask you.'

'Which chemist does it say on the label?' I couldn't remember.

'I haven't got them here,' she snapped. 'They're still with the lab. They'll be notifying the police as a matter of course.'

'The police?'

'Christ, yes. This sort of slipshod practice just isn't on. These are powerful drugs being dished out by some incompetent pharmacist who shouldn't be allowed to make up lucky bags, let alone medicines. I've left my name as a contact seeing as I sent the sample in but I'd better check with you I've got the facts right.'

We went over dates and times, names and places until Moira was clear about the sequence of events that had led to me leaving the tablets with her.

It was ironic really. If the scan that Mr Simcock had done hadn't shown advanced organic changes to Lily's brain then Agnes' early suspicions that her decline was too rapid and could be due to some external factors could have been spot on. The high dosage and the combination of drugs would be enough to make anyone demented, Moira had said. Take her off the medication and the symptoms will go. It seemed terribly unfair that Lily actually had Alzheimer's. I needed to tell Agnes about Moira's news, although given the outlook for Lily and her current illness I thought there'd be cold comfort in the knowledge that there had been something amiss with the thioridazine tablets.

Something else niggled too. Goulden's reaction to the tablets going missing. Was it simply overzealous housekeeping or had he realised there was something wrong with them? Maybe he'd simply never got round to reducing the dosage as he'd promised us, and was covering his tracks. Or perhaps he'd realised there'd been some big cock-up at the chemists and didn't want anyone to know. Why? No skin off his nose, surely. If he wanted to protect his own reputation as a doctor it'd be in his interests to have the chemist struck off for such negligence.

I wondered what Mrs Knight, the matron's, part in all this was. She who lied about the retrieval of the bottle. What had prompted that? Had Goulden confided in her? I checked the clock. Ray was collecting Maddie and Tom, Friday afternoon being an early finish, in the time-honoured tradition of the building trade. If I set off now I could probably catch Mrs Knight before she left for home.

CHAPTER TWENTY-TWO

I cycled round to Homelea. Heavy cloud cover threatened squalls of rain and made it dark for late afternoon. Homelea was a picture of warmth and welcome. Cheery yellow light spilled from the large bay windows, and as I locked my bike at the side, two women in wheelchairs, laden with shopping bags, were pushed up the ramp by young assistants.

Inside I could smell onions and a whiff of roasting fat before my nose clogged up again. It was a busy time of day with residents congregating downstairs for afternoon tea and staff preparing the dining room for the evening meal. In the general hubbub no one asked me my business.

I followed the corridor round and knocked twice on the office door while twisting the handle. I heard a faint 'Come in.' I opened the door. Mrs Knight was at the desk. She looked up in enquiry, then as she recognised me her face twisted with dismay before she had a chance to mask it.

'Mrs Knight, we need to talk.'

'I don't see what...' She rose, flustered.

'Don't you?' I spoke sharply. 'It's about Lily Palmer. And those tablets she was given.'

'I don't have to listen to this.' She was outraged. 'I don't know who you think you are, barging in here, taking that tone.'

'I'm a private detective,' I said. I sat in the chair opposite her.

She remained standing, her palms braced on the edge of the desk. She stared at me, her mouth slightly agape.

'My client was concerned about the care that Mrs Palmer was receiving here – with good cause, it seems.'

'What are you implying?' She rallied. 'Our residents are well looked after, we're inspected regularly by Social Services. We've never had any complaints. If you wish to make a complaint I suggest you contact the local authority, but I can assure you–'

'The tablets that went missing,' I persisted. 'There was something different about them, wasn't there?'

She frowned. 'They were a different brand, that's all,' she said dismissively.

'Oh, just a different brand? So any of the patients could have had them?'

'Well, no. We always keep individual prescriptions separate, to ensure we can monitor the course. It reduces the risk of giving anyone the wrong medication.'

'Why did you lie about the missing bottle turning up again?'

'I didn't – one of the girls found them, like I said.'

I shook my head slowly. 'They can't have done. I know. I've got the tablets.'

She clasped her hands together. 'What?... You took them?'

'They were found in Lily's slippers. I don't think anyone deliberately stole them. Why did you lie about them being found?'

There were a couple of beats while she weighed up whether to confess. She took a deep breath. 'It was important to reassure people that there'd been no negligence. Dr Goulden was very clear about that.'

'He told you to say they'd turned up?'

'He said it could reflect very badly on us here. There's a very strict check kept on the medicines.' She mumbled something else, her head lowered, the neat black cap of hair swinging forward to hide her expression.

'Pardon?'

'He said he would see to the paperwork.'

'You didn't think it was strange? Such concern about one small bottle of tablets?'

'In the wrong hands–'

'But he was very agitated about it, wasn't he? He virtually accused Miss Donlan of stealing them. He had a go at you.'

'He has a short temper,' she couldn't bring herself to be critical, 'he'd had a bad night.' She shrugged her shoulders.

'Mrs Knight, where did you usually get prescriptions made up?'

'The chemist round the corner.'

'But these were different?'

She frowned. 'Yes, the doctor brought them himself. They often get samples from the drug companies. He said we might as well try them, they were the right prescription for Mrs Palmer and they'd probably work out cheaper in the long run. I really don't know why you're making such a song and dance about it. And if you've got the tablets,' she said briskly, 'then they can be returned and everything can be straightened out.' She gave me a bright look.

'I'm afraid I can't do that,' I said. 'You see, there was something wrong with those tablets.'

'Wrong? What do you mean?'

'They were four times the stated dosage. Lily Palmer was being given huge amounts of thioridazine – enough to make her very poorly. She'd become more agitated and confused, she'd have trouble sleeping. And every time she was given something to help her sleep it would react with the high level of drugs and increase her confusion. She was aggressive the night she was admitted to hospital, wasn't she, stumbling about, hallucinating, thinking people were trying to harm her?'

'Oh, my goodness.' She sank into her chair. Her shock seemed genuine.

'We've had them analysed. They definitely contain the wrong amount of the drug.'

'Oh, my goodness,' she repeated. 'It's the sort of accident you dread. How on earth could it...' She didn't finish her question, her thoughts leaping ahead. 'Surely we couldn't be liable. We gave them in good faith. There was no negligence here. The label had the wrong dosage on – how could we possibly know?'

'I don't know which chemist made them up,' I said.

'They were from Malden's,' she said. 'Malden Medical Supplies – we deal with them for all our regular stock: dressings, Zimmer frames, disposables – that sort of thing. When I saw the tablets I remember being surprised because I didn't know they did pharmaceuticals too. I assumed it was a new departure.'

Malden's. I was surprised too, but I needed to concentrate on getting as much from Mrs Knight as I could while she was still reeling from the news I'd given her.

'What about Ernest Theakston?'

'Sorry?' She narrowed her eyes as if to focus her hearing.

'Ernest Theakston, he was here until he got transferred to Kingsfield. What medication was he on?'

'I don't know.' She riffled through the card index on her desk and then stood up and opened the top drawer of the filing cabinet and pulled out another batch of file cards.

'Was he on thioridazine too? Or anything from a different chemist?'

She found the card and scanned it. 'No.' She looked across at me puzzled. What was I getting at?

220

'Mrs Palmer's tablets, they were the first time Dr Goulden had supplied them directly?'

'I'm not sure,' she said. 'Now and again he'll give us a free sample. Like I said, he gets so much from the reps.'

'But not in the case of Mr Theakston?'

'No.'

'And you've not had any drugs from Malden's before?'

'No.'

'How long was Mr Theakston here?'

'Four years.' Nothing like the quick sojourn that Lily had made.

'And why did he go into Kingsfield?'

'He'd deteriorated. Dr Goulden wanted an assessment.'

'Deteriorated? In what way? What was wrong with him?'

'Alzheimer's. We can cope with the early stages but when it really progresses and they need twenty-four-hour care there's better provision elsewhere.'

'What happened to Mr Theakston?'

'I don't know.'

It was frustrating. I'd anticipated some dramatic pattern linking the fate of Lily Palmer and Ernest Theakston but their histories seemed quite distinct. Ernest Theakston, like some of the people from Aspen Lodge, had stayed several years in the home before going to the Marion Unit and he'd not had any dodgy drugs.

She obviously didn't know about Goulden's connection with Malden's and I wasn't going to enlighten her.

'This is awful,' she said. 'We certainly won't want to use them in future, not for anything like that. This is just ... awful.' She put away the cards and returned to her desk. 'What's Dr Goulden said? He must be furious.'

'I haven't spoken to him yet.'

'Oh dear. I'll have to tell Mrs Valley-Brown. Look,' she swallowed and swung back her hair, 'what I said, about the tablets being found again, that doesn't need to come out, does it? I'd no idea then ... I was just following Dr Goulden's advice. If I'd known...'

And if he'd said jump off a cliff? I didn't reply. She coloured.

'I'll see myself out.'

The clouds had opened and gusts of wind made cycling a feat of endurance. The battery in my back light had gone all weedy and I prayed the weak red glow was visible to the cars that raced past me.

Somewhere in the darker corners of my

imagination I'd been expecting to uncover some major systematic crime – Goulden doing nasty things with drugs to his patients. But Ernest Theakston didn't fit my theory. He hadn't had any medication to speak of. One of the other patients, Philip Braithwaite from Aspen Lodge, the one with the brain tumour, he'd been on something, I could remember his daughter telling me.

So what? I kept coming back to the bloody great hole in the argument – why? What possible reason could there be for making people ill instead of well? For kicks? Stories like that hit the press every so often but it was a pretty remote possibility. I should find out what had happened to Ernest Theakston. Maybe that would shed some light on things, connect what had happened to him with Lily's situation, or with Malden Medical Supplies.

The most plausible scenario so far was that someone at Malden's had ballsed up the prescription.

And the most Ken Goulden could be accused of was nepotism, a short temper and failure to recognise an adverse reaction to the medicines he'd prescribed. But something else about the Malden's link hovered just beyond my consciousness. I tried to focus on it, something Harry had mentioned when he'd given me the information, a little thing... It was no good, I couldn't bring it into view.

I was sure Mrs Knight had known nothing about the link between the doctor and Malden's or that there was any problem with the drugs. She hadn't tried to hide anything. She'd been stunned by my revelations. Her fear for her own reputation, fear of litigation, were at the forefront, not a fear of being found out. Strange woman, prickly but obviously scared of Goulden – and how odd the way she never smiled. Why had she gone into nursing? She didn't seem particularly caring of people. For all her shock-horror expressions of concern she'd never once asked me how Lily Palmer was.

CHAPTER TWENTY-THREE

Nana Tello had come for tea. She was holding court in the kitchen as I walked in. Sheila, Maddie and Tom were at the table. Ray was at the cooker.

'Hello, stranger,' she interrupted her story to greet me. 'You been on your bike?'

'Yes.' I peeled off my cagoule.

She shook her head, tutted, pulled a face. 'It's not safe. I don't think it's so good. The cars these days, they are so impatient.'

It was a fair comment but given the history of our relationship it felt as though she were criticising my recklessness in still cycling rather than anything. else.

'They have no manners, no courtesy.' She grimaced her disapproval.

'I can curtsy, look.' Maddie leapt up and performed a jerky bob. Sheila and Ray burst out laughing.

'I'll have a wash,' I muttered, and withdrew.

When I tried to ring Agnes there was no reply. She was probably visiting Lily.

Tea was a strained affair. Ray had made a baked aubergine dish which only Sheila and I enjoyed. Maddie declared it was like 'slugs and blood' and refused to try it. Tom followed suit. Meanwhile Nana Tello embarked on her customary discourse on the need for meat (red meat at that) in the human diet, especially for young children. I'd been through the argument with her before, as had Ray, but she still managed to needle him.

'Come on, Ma,' he said. 'How many times a week could people back home afford meat?

They didn't have it every day, did they?'

'Can we get chips?' Maddie whined.

'No,' I said.

'Aw. Please. Be your best friend. Please.'

'No. If you don't want this then you can have a sandwich.'

'There's beans,' Ray offered.

'I hate beans,' Maddie announced with passion.

'Since when?'

'I hate beans too,' Tom said.

'No, you don't, you're just copying me. Copycat, copycat, you don't know what you're looking at.'

'Sandwich, then.' I got up and made a round of Marmite sandwiches. I wasn't even going to introduce the option of what particular type of sandwiches were acceptable on this particular Friday.

Sheila had managed to steer Nana Tello off meat and on to Italy. Sheila had spent several holidays there and was extolling the delights of the different regions she'd visited. Nana Tello was beside herself with joy to find that Sheila knew her home town of Reggio Calabria and went off into long rhapsodies about the market, the churches, the people, the climate, the soil and the schools.

We made it through apple pie and ice

cream and coffee without further tantrums.

Later, comfortably ensconced in the pub, I let Diane's conversation and two pints of Boddies wash away my tension. Diane was still full of the Cornerhouse exhibition and a little daunted by the amount of work she needed to do for it. 'And I've got to write one of those awful little autobiographies too. For the catalogue. That's the pits,' she said. 'Can you imagine it? What do you say? What do you leave out?'

'What do other people say?'

'Well,' she ran her hands through her hair, which had become a savage blue-black since we'd last met, 'some of them go on about where they've trained, who's influenced their work, then there's the "loves crochet – lives with six cats" style...'

'You could stick in a bit of both.'

'It's so difficult, you've no idea. I spent three hours last night trying to come up with something but everything sounded either totally boring or horribly pretentious.'

'How long does it have to be?' I took another satisfying swallow of beer.

'They said up to two hundred words.'

'You could try keeping it really short.'

'What, like "Diane Davis lives in Rus-holme"?'

I grinned.

'What do people really want to know?' She threw her hands wide as she asked the question. 'I mean, if you go to an exhibition, you can see the work, what more would you want to know about the artist?'

I thought for a moment, took a swig from my glass, frowned in concentration. 'How many cats they've got and if they do crochet.'

'Sod off.'

Over our next drink I told Diane about the case of the dodgy tablets.

'Someone's for the high jump then. What a cock-up. Reminds me of those awful stories about keeping weedkiller in pop bottles.'

'Oh, don't,' I muttered.

'Bit embarrassing, eh? Use the family firm and they give you seriously shoddy goods. You reckon this doctor's in on it, then?'

'I'm sure he is, but it's just a gut feeling. I can't find a reason for him to be deliberately overdosing patients, in fact some of the patients he had transferred to Kingsfield weren't even on medication. He seems to have pretty easy access for his patients to the Marion Unit there – his brother-in-law is the consultant.'

'All in the family. You scratch my back and I'll scratch yours?'

'Possibly. You wouldn't think they could get away with it, what with all these reforms and the Patient's Charter and all that. And the bottom line is the woman's got advanced Alzheimer's anyway. She was ill in spite of the tablets, not because of them.'

'But they can't have helped.'

'Oh, no. Moira reckoned they would have made anyone demented, especially when mixed with other drugs.'

'Do you think he'll get away with it, then, that sort of negligence?'

I nodded. 'Unless something else crops up he's home free. Everything points to the chemist, who will probably be suspended or whatever they do. I don't think there's much to be done about the doctor using samples from Malden's – free market and all that. Anyway the police are looking into it now. And I need to find some more work.'

'You could run an ad again,' Diane suggested.

'Yeah. It's about time I did something like that.'

'Hey, you could make one of those ads for the cinema, you know, stick it in with the ones about local jewellers and car dealers.'

'Oh, spare me, please.'

'Or one of those videos they show in taxis,'

she cackled, 'or a bulletin on the Internet.'

'You need a computer first,' I replied, 'and seeing as neither of us has one...'

'I'm going to get one.'

I stared at her.

'Yep, CD ROM, colour printer, the lot, fax as well.'

'Bloody hell.'

'My own personal technological revolution. You ought to think about it, Sal, you'll get left behind.'

'Yeah, yeah. Besides, I have thought about it, like window-shopping. I just can't afford it.'

'When you win the Lottery...'

'Hah!' I sneered. 'You have to play to win. I never play, thought you knew that. Even if I did I've more chance of flying to outer space than winning that.'

'But just think, all the things you could do with a good system, with so much less effort.'

'I know. I know, technology's a wonderful thing. Take my answerphone...'

'Sal!' she complained.

'Listen. My answerphone got someone off a murder charge.' I told her about Jimmy Achebe's alibi, how it fixed him in time and place.

'But how did they know he wasn't ringing

from home,' she asked, 'pretending he was at work?'

'Ah! Because you could hear the yard in the background, all these vans and a Tannoy, really clear. It was brilliant. It proved he was at work, miles away at about the time of the murder. And now it looks like they're on to the right suspect.'

We nattered on some more about what we liked and didn't about the new technology.

'Promise me,' said Diane, 'if I ever get obsessive about it, you'll tell me.'

'Promise.'

'Hey, maybe you could be the first virtual private eye, shadowing people down the Information Superhighway, uncovering virtual crime.'

'What, for virtual money? Give over.'

I slept late on the Saturday morning. My cold was receding and I'd enough energy to make a start on planting up the cold frame. Maddie and I made a trip to the local garden centre and bought a selection of packets of seeds. I limited myself to petunias and lobelia for tubs and baskets, I could supplement them with cuttings I'd taken from ivy and pansies. I got some asters for the border and Maddie chose lettuce and candytuft for herself and Tom.

On the way back I called at the office to check my mail. There was a handwritten envelope. I didn't recognise the writing. I opened it eagerly though I should have realised that no friend would write to me at my work address. Inside was a cheque, drawn on the account of Mr J. W. Achebe. Jimmy, paying off his debt. The fact he'd bothered to sort it out in the midst of what he must be going through brought a lump to my throat. There was a small note with it; it just read 'Thank you.' I sighed, put it in my drawer to deal with on Monday. Poor Jimmy. Now he was free to start grieving for the loss of Tina. There'd be all the arrangements to make for her funeral once they released the body. He'd been transformed from murderer to widower. Had friends and family believed him guilty, how would they ever face him again?

It was a mild, grey day and the two of us pottered nicely, filling old seed trays with compost, sprinkling on seeds, watering them gently and putting them in the frame.

Maddie wanted a picnic lunch so I heated a tin of soup and we sipped it from mugs, along with cheese rolls. She chattered on about school, mainly about Miss Bryan, her teacher, who she was deeply in love with. She wanted to be exactly like Miss Bryan, she was going to be a teacher like Miss Bryan, Miss Bryan had three earrings in one ear. I watched a magpie pulling twigs from a tree in the adjoining garden and flying off with them.

I left Maddie playing with her bike and went in to ring Moira. What had happened with the police?

'They got the gist of it over the phone,' she said, 'then they sent a chap round last night, had to repeat it all again. Said it'd be Monday at least before they'd be doing anything – no point in calling on people over the weekend. Not a high priority for them, anyway.'

I rang Agnes too. Lily was neither better nor worse. They thought it was pneumonia. Agnes had been there the previous evening. I told her what the results were on the tablets.

'I knew there was something wrong with them.' She was triumphant. 'I just knew it. Four times too strong. It really is disgraceful. How did it happen? Did he write out a faulty prescription?'

'No, the label's got the correct dosage on – it's the tablets that are stronger than the label says. You'd only know that if you had them analysed. The mistake must have been made when they were being prepared.'

'It's a clear case of negligence, isn't it?' she said. 'Whoever's got it wrong must be disciplined.'

'Well, the police are involved now. My friend the GP who sent them to the lab had to report it so they'll hopefully get to the bottom of it. But listen to this, they were made up at Malden's, the place where Mrs Goulden works. I think Goulden's covering up because Malden's got it wrong. I bet he didn't do anything after we went to see him, thought we were cranks, and now he's realised... The others probably know too. It could ruin them, bad publicity and that, endangering life. But, Agnes, I think there's more to it than just the tablets.'

'Yes?'

'I don't believe it's just a coincidence that all these people are involved, both in the firm and in Lily's case. I'm not that gullible. I talked to Mrs Knight and I'm sure she knew nothing about it, she was completely fazed when I told her about the dosage, and she only lied about the tablets turning up because Goulden had bullied her into it. But I checked on Ernest Theakston – the other resident from Homelea who'd gone to Kingsfield this year. His case was totally different from Lily's. He'd been ill for a long time, the progress of the disease was slow and he never had any medication from Malden's. I can't see any motive either. Just suppose we're right, there's something going on, Goulden gets funny tablets made up at his wife's lab, gives them to Lily, who's got dementia anyway. She becomes even more demented, they can't control her so she's referred to Montgomery for assessment at Kingsfield.'

'Then she falls,' Agnes spoke calmly, 'if she did fall.'

I thought of the other patient with her riddles about the fall. Was she pushed? They wouldn't dare, would they? But no one had seen her fall, neither Mrs Li nor the nurse we'd seen. Who'd found her or seen it happen?

'All right – if she did fall. So she has an operation to sort out the bleeding in her brain.'

'She gets an infection.'

'But apparently unrelated to the operation or the medication.'

There was a pause. We'd reached the end of the story so far.

'Why?' I said. 'What's it all for?'

'I've no idea,' said Agnes, 'but I wasn't

born yesterday. I think you should tell the police everything you've found out, let them deal with it.'

I had my doubts, but rang off promising Agnes I'd contact the police.

CHAPTER TWENTY-FOUR

Back in the garden I set to weeding and rehearsed what I could tell the police. It didn't amount to anything they'd want to hear – a mishmash of connections, suspicions and concerns. The only hard evidence of any wrongdoing was the falsely labelled pills, and the police were already looking into that.

I struggled with a crop of dandelions along the edge of the flagged path. It wasn't a crime for a GP to be eager to refer patients to a well-regarded local psycho-geriatric unit, even if his brother-in-law did work there. It wasn't a crime for the same GP to order drugs from his wife's pharmaceutical company or for the city's neurosurgeon to sit on the board of that company. It wasn't a crime for a GP to lose his temper.

I was right. There were too many coincidences for comfort. But I wasn't going to go making a fool of myself in front of the police. Let them look into the mix-up with the tablets, meanwhile I needed more idea of how this all connected to Lily Palmer. Suppose she had been pushed – she was very ill now in hospital – did somebody want Lily dead? I threw down the trowel, washed the soil off my hands and rang Agnes back.

'Did you ever check whether Charles was the only beneficiary in Lily's will?'

'No.'

'Can you check for me, find out where the will's held and if she made any recent changes?'

'I can do. He's up for the weekend, I'll be seeing him at the hospital. You think that might be behind it all? Lily only had the house, nothing else. That was sold off so there would be enough to pay the charges at Homelea.'

'And she wasn't there very long so there'd be quite a lot still left. I'm sorry, it's a horrible thought, but I think we should check.'

'But Charles would contest it, if there was anything like that, surely.'

'Let's wait and see what he says.'

I was filling the watering can when the

doorbell rang. If I'd been back out in the garden I probably wouldn't have heard it.

Dr Ken Goulden was on the doorstep. My stomach lurched. I wanted to run. How the hell had he got my home address? He was bigger than I remembered, built like a rugby player.

'What do you want?' I was hardly civil.

'Just what do you think you're playing at?'

I opened my mouth but it was a rhetorical question.

'I don't know what your game is, Miss Kilkenny, but you've been making wild allegations, upsetting staff at Homelea and interfering in business that doesn't concern you.' His jaw was taut as he reined in his temper.

'But it does concern me,' I replied. 'It concerns me a great deal actually. Mrs Palmer was being given enough drugs to make–'

'You've no right to go around meddling in medical affairs,' he said fiercely. 'You stay away from my patients, is that clear?'

'Those tablets were dangerous,' I retorted. 'Doesn't that concern you?'

'Mummy, who is it?' Maddie called from the kitchen.

'Just someone from work. You go back in the garden.'

'I want a drink.'

'I'll be there in a minute.'

'Mistakes happen, human error,' Goulden said. 'It's regrettable but that's no reason for this sort of vindictive harassment. I'll be speaking to my solicitor. I have a reputation to think about and I'm not going to let you jeopardise that with your cheap innuendo and your wild accusations.'

Bloody hell! What on earth had Mrs Knight said to him? 'I work with facts,' I began, my anger mounting. 'You prescribed those drugs, your wife's firm supplied them and when we came to you worried about Mrs Palmer you did nothing—'

He didn't let me carry on. 'You stay away from my patients.' He pushed his finger at me, emphasising the words. 'Any more harassment...'

'Mummy?' Maddie was coming down the hall.

I moved to go in. Goulden grabbed my wrist, his hand large and hot. 'Do you understand?' he hissed at me. I could smell whisky on his breath. It mingled with a citrus aftershave. 'Any more meddling from you, missy, and my brief will be down on you like a ton of bricks. We'll do you for theft, trespass, defamation, libel, the works. Your feet won't touch the ground.' His nostrils whitened and his cheeks reddened as he spoke. 'You can kiss goodbye to all this.' He jerked his head towards the house. 'You won't know what's hit you.'

'Let go.' I enunciated clearly through clenched teeth.

He dropped my wrist and I moved inside, slammed the door shut. My wrist ached. I was as livid as I was scared. The arrogant, bullying bastard. To come here and threaten me. Just wait, I thought. The police will soon be knocking on your door, matey, asking awkward questions.

'Why was that man and you shouting?'

I steered Maddie back to the kitchen. 'We were having an argument about work. He's gone now. So, you want a drink?'

'Blackcurrant.'

I unscrewed the lid. My hand was shaking so much it was all I could do to pour the dark syrup into the cup.

On Sunday Agnes rang me. Lily's will was in Charles' safekeeping. She'd updated it just before her move to Homelea so it would take account of the change in her circumstances. Charles was the sole beneficiary.

'We've put the wind up Goulden,' I said. I

240

told her about his unwelcome visit. 'I don't think he's realised that the police have been informed. I'd love to see his face when they turn up on the doorstep.'

'Sal, hadn't you better talk to them soon, if he's been to your home, threatening you?'

'I will.'

Then I rang Moira to find out who was handling the investigation.

'DS Wignall – you can get hold of him at Bootle Street. Won't be there today. Why?'

'I'd like to talk to him. There's a lot of questions that could do with looking into. I've had Dr Goulden round, telling me to lay off.'

'Really?'

'Oh, yes. Got quite nasty.'

'Sal, you didn't tell him about the police?'

'No. But he knows about the lab results.'

'How?'

I felt sheepish. 'Well, I went to see the matron at the home, after I'd spoken to you on Friday. I didn't mention the police or anything. Anyway, she must have told Goulden.'

'Well, I shouldn't think DS Wignall will be best pleased.'

'Maybe not, but I don't think Goulden realises how far it's gone. He's not about to flee the country or anything. As far as he's concerned I've had an analysis done which threatened his precious reputation and he came to warn me off.'

Maddie and I spent a couple of hours sorting out the toy boxes. While she rediscovered lost treasures I ended up reuniting Lego, removing rotting fragments of crisps and apple and chucking obscure bits of plastic and broken toys in the bin when I was sure she wasn't looking. It all looked neater and cleaner when we finished. It was now possible to tell which box held jigsaws and games and which was Duplo and other little figures. It'd stay like that for all of forty-eight hours until Tom and Maddie had time to redistribute it all thoroughly.

By then I was ready to put my feet up. There was a feature in the Sunday paper which highlighted the shortage of NHS beds for people with Alzheimer's and the lack of psycho-geriatric units. Most people were being cared for in private homes, many staffed by inexperienced workers. Manchester and the Marion Unit was one of the examples. A local GP was quoted: 'It's now virtually impossible to refer a patient to the Marion Unit and have any hope of their getting a place. There's a ridiculous waiting list. The unit only has sixty beds, twenty-five of those are for acute cases and short-term stay where people need to see a consultant and have proper assessment. We've a growing elderly population and shrinking resources. No one's suggesting a return to the old days of the large psychiatric hospitals but we desperately need more facilities. It's an intolerable situation.'

But Dr Goulden managed to get his patients in, six in one year. It stank.

First thing Monday morning I rang the registry office, got put through to deaths and gave them Ernest Theakston's name and date of birth. Asked them to search for a death in the last six months. Normally they want you to make a written application, or go in and spend hours there yourself searching through index cards, but with recent deaths they can call them up on the computer.

He was there. He'd died at the Manchester Royal Infirmary, about ten days after he'd left Homelea.

'I can't verify that for you,' said the clerk. 'You'd need to come in for verification.'

'No, it's OK,' I said. 'That's him. I'm sure that's him.'

I didn't know what had killed him. But it sure as hell wasn't old age.

CHAPTER TWENTY-FIVE

Lily died that Sunday night. Agnes rang me midmorning. The hospital had notified Charles and he'd let her know. The pneumonia had failed to respond to the antibiotics.

'I want to go see her,' said Agnes, her voice remarkably firm.

'I'll take you,' I volunteered. 'I'll be there soon.'

I tried Bootle Street before leaving, but DS Wignall was out.

The sun glanced off the wet road, making me squint as I drove. I fished in the glove compartment for my sunglasses. They were there in amongst half-empty packets of crisps and tourist leaflets.

Agnes smiled when she opened the door. She was impeccably turned out, white hair carefully brushed, a touch of lipstick, small navy studs in her ears which matched her coat. 'Thank you for coming. I could probably have managed on the buses but all that waiting around is so tiring.'

'It's all right,' I said. 'I wanted to come.'

Once in the car Agnes began to discuss the funeral arrangements. Charles had already organised that. 'It'll be Southern Cemetery, the crematorium. She always wanted her ashes on the rose garden. That's where they took Olive, her daughter. That was March too. Easter time.' She seemed remarkably composed. If my closest friend, Diane, had just died I'd have been in bits. Did emotions dull with age? Had Agnes prepared herself for this or was she still in shock at the news?

We were just turning into the hospital car park when she spoke again. 'Have you talked to the police?'

'Not yet. I tried to get through this morning but the person I need to talk to wasn't there. I wish we had something more substantial to go on, some sort of evidence to give them. A crime to report.'

'Lily's dead.' Measured voice.

'Yes, and the cause of death will be bronchial pneumonia. It's very common amongst old people, isn't it? Harder to fight infection.'

'So no one will think twice about it.'

'Only us.' I climbed out of the car.

'Sal,' she stood beside the passenger door, 'you will keep trying, won't you? You will talk to the police?' She wasn't pleading and her gaze was steady.

'Yes. But don't hold out too much hope.' I locked the car. 'They can investigate the tablets but the rest may just sound like we're being paranoid. You know, we could ask about a post-mortem, on the grounds that the excessive medication might have contributed to her death.'

'Yes.' She was decisive. 'Who do we ask?'

'I don't know. We'll find out.'

We arrived at the ward and explained at the nurses' station that we'd heard about Lily Palmer, we wanted to see her. Consternation. Glances flew between them and there was an awkward pause. The tallest nurse blushed but took charge of the situation.

'I'm afraid we didn't realise you'd be coming in today. Mrs Palmer's been moved already.'

'To the funeral home?' Agnes asked.

'No, she's still here at the hospital.' She cleared her throat. 'She carried a donor card. We have permission to use her organs for medical research. I'm sorry,' she looked at each of us, 'you shouldn't need to think about it at a time like this. But I'm sure you'll be able to see her. Take a seat in the waiting room and I'll ring round and find out where she is.'

'We want to know if we can have a post-mortem done.'

'Really?' She looked startled. 'That's not usual where it's a death due to natural causes.'

'But if we want it done – who do we have to see?'

'Let me check for you.'

We sat in the TV lounge, which was mercifully empty. The minutes ticked by. Agnes closed her eyes. I got up and went for a wander up and down the corridor, reading the notices. In the background the curious cheer that's endemic to places of illness rang out in the calls and comments of staff and patients. There was the clatter of a dinner trolley making its rounds. The scent of onion and cauliflower wafted through the building. I went back and joined Agnes.

The tall nurse appeared. 'Sorry to keep you waiting. We should be able to go down now. You asked about the post-mortem. Now the certificate was issued giving a natural cause of death, she didn't die during surgery, as the result of a fall or anything like that, so you'll need to talk to the coroner and explain why you want a post-mortem, and of course the next of kin will have to give their permission. I've notified pathology to wait until they hear

247

before they do anything else.'

I asked her about Lily's personal belongings.

'Her son said he'd pick them up on Friday when he comes back up for the funeral. I'm so sorry about the mix-up. You can see her now. If you'll come this way.'

We took the lift up and walked the length of the corridor before taking another lift down to the basement. On the way the nurse commiserated with Agnes. 'I don't know if it helps but it was very peaceful. There was no pain. She just stopped breathing.'

We turned left through double doors: the pathology department. The nurse led us to a door on the right. She opened it and we filed into the small anteroom. In the centre, on a trolley, lay Lily. Her face was soft in death. They'd removed her glasses, folded her arms across her chest. She wore a white hospital gown, a sheet covered her from the chest down and a towel was tucked round the back and sides of her head. There was no sign that they'd started recovering bits from her body. Thank God they hadn't been halfway through removing her eyes or something.

I looked again at her arms. The arms that had held her daughter, Olive, in birth and death. The sentiment caught me unawares, tears prickled my nose. I swallowed hard, touched Agnes on the arm. 'I'll wait outside.' This was her bereavement.

There was nowhere to sit in the corridor so I paced up and down for a bit. Double doors at the end led to the pathology labs and adjacent double doors to an outside yard, delivery area and wheelie bins. Presumably this was where the vehicles came to take bodies away to the funeral parlours. I was leaning against the corridor wall when the doors from the lab swung open. A young man in a white coat swept through and out of the doors to the yard.

I followed. I caught the whiff of tobacco smoke. He inhaled deeply, leaning back against the brick wall. He looked a little startled when he saw me, straightened up.

I smiled. 'Hi! They ought to give you a smokers' room.'

'They have,' he dragged again, 'it's miles away.'

'And too smoky?'

He laughed. 'Right.'

'Do you work in the lab?'

He nodded, blew out smoke.

'I've brought my neighbour in to see her friend, died last night. They'd already moved her down here. Bit embarrassing really. She's an organ donor. When you do that do they use everything?'

He shrugged. 'Depends. Some organs go for transplants, kidneys and that. They take those in theatre. Or there might be some research going on so there's a demand for something particular. Like last year there was someone doing some stuff on livers, they wanted lots of whole livers.'

'Do they do it here, the research?'

'Some. Lot of stuff goes off to other centres, some abroad, research labs. Depends.'

'What sort of thing would they take from Mrs Palmer?'

He looked uncomfortable, looked away. 'I don't know if that's...'

'I'm sorry. Bit ghoulish, isn't it!' I giggled, trying to play up the chatterbox character. 'Just thought with her being old perhaps they can't use much.'

'She had Alzheimer's, didn't she?'

I nodded. So did he.

'They've got her down for the brain.'

Of course.

'They've still no way of treating it, still trying to work out why it develops. Lot of research going on all over the place. Like AIDS,' he said. 'Whoever finds the cure, they're going to make millions. Big bucks.'

'Do they do that here as well?' I asked. 'I'm so nosy,' I added, 'but my mum always used to say, "Don't ask – never know".'

'I think they do some here but this is going to some private lab they use in Cheshire.'

'Malden's!'

Suspicion clouded his face.

'My cousin works there, research. What a small world, honestly! It's always happening.' I rattled on inanely. 'I went on holiday last year – Corfu – and who turns out to be in the next apartment but someone from primary school. Amazing. Well, I'd better get back.' I must have come across as either crass or suspect but it didn't matter. Lily Palmer was dead and Malden's were expecting her brain. It just added to the stench surrounding the whole affair.

I returned to wait outside the anteroom. The smoker came in a couple of minutes later. He glanced my way. I grinned and waved like an old friend. He smiled weakly. I guessed he was probably regretting answering my questions but wasn't worried enough to do anything about my snooping; Probably chalked me up as a typical nosy parker.

Agnes emerged from the anteroom pale but dry-eyed.

251

'Has the nurse gone?' she asked.

'Yes.'

'It feels strange, leaving her alone with no one to watch over...' She broke off for a moment, her hand crept to the brooch on her lapel and fussed with it. 'That's what we used to do, you know, when the bodies were laid out at home. You'd keep the candles lit and take turns sitting up with them. It was part of life. That sounds silly, doesn't it, death being part of life, but it was. Not like this.' She gestured at the corridor. 'People wanted to be at home. There was always a neighbour who knew how to prepare the body, she'd come in and you'd help. It was so natural. Nowadays you never hear of it, do you? People would be shocked, wouldn't they? It's all left to the professionals now.'

When she finished she stood there, trim in her smart coat and slightly bewildered.

'Come on,' I said, 'time to go.'

CHAPTER TWENTY-SIX

I nearly collided with Jimmy Achebe leaving the hospital. I don't know who was more surprised.

'Jimmy!'

He looked startled, poised to run, until he realised who I was. We both spoke at the same time.

'How are you?' I asked. 'I'm so sorry...'

'I've sent a cheque,' he blurted out.

We both stopped, embarrassed.

'Yes, thank you. I got it on Saturday. About Tina...'

He looked away, ill at ease, dropped his cigarette and ground it out, pushed his hands into the pockets of his jacket. I was aware of Agnes moving a little bit further away from us.

'I'm so sorry. It must be awful, and to be held at the police station on top of everything else...'

He nodded briskly, sniffed and hunched his shoulders against the cold. 'Yeah,' he said quietly.

'I saw in the paper, about the charges. Do you know when it'll come to court?'

He shook his head again. 'They don't tell me anything.' He raised his eyes to mine. They were shiny, blazing with hurt. He shuddered.

I couldn't think of anything to say but it seemed abrupt to leave it like that. He spoke first.

'Better go, visiting my mum,' he explained. He nodded towards the entrance. 'She's in for tests – and now with all this...' He left the sentence hanging. The murder of a daughter-in-law would be devastating, even for someone in good health, but to have your son all but accused of killing her into the bargain – horrendous.

'I am sorry,' I repeated. 'Bye, Jimmy.'

He dipped his head in reply and wheeled away through the doors and back into the brightly lit corridor. He seemed eager to go. Did he think hiring me had set in motion the chain of events that had led to Tina's death? Had it? It wasn't a question I could ask. I'd have to wait for Bill Sherwin's trial to see if it was answered. But had that association made him uncomfortable with me or was it just the sheer bloody pain of grief and the awkwardness between people who don't know how to share it?

I didn't say anything to Agnes about Jimmy and she was discreet enough not to ask. We made our way back to the car. The sun still shone but the bitter wind cut right through my clothing. It was a relief to get into the car.

'Did you find anything out?' She fastened her seat belt.

I hesitated. Would it be insensitive to tell her?

'Please don't spare me the details,' she said sharply. 'Lily's dead now, she's at peace, nothing else can hurt her. The least I can do is find out whether her death was inevitable.'

'They're going to remove her brain. It's going to be sent to Malden's for research.'

'Malden's again. What is going on, Sal?'

I sighed. 'I don't know. You need to ring Charles and get him to agree to a post-mortem. I can't see he'd object, with what we know about the pills. And that's what I'll tell the coroner – that we know she was given very high dosages and we want to see if it contributed to her death. I'll try the police again too.'

There was a bank statement waiting for me

at the office along with another exhortation to take out a loan. Hell, they just wanted to get me deeper in debt. Kilkenny Investigations was hardly in a position to pay the bills, never mind a loan.

I got out the Achebe file, made a note of the payment from Jimmy. Clean slate. I put the cheque in my bag to deposit at the bank.

I trembled. The office was freezing. I'd no fresh milk. Sod it, I could do my other calls from home either side of collecting Maddie and Tom.

I rang the police. DS Wignall was out of the office and would return my call when he got back.

The coroner was in. He listened to my concerns. I concentrated solely on the medication Lily had been receiving, and he agreed a post-mortem should be held. 'We're always happy to arrange a post-mortem in a case like this, set people's minds at rest.'

Or set them thinking.

He needed to hear from next of kin, though, for permission. Meanwhile he would confirm with the hospital that the body was to be held in the morgue until further notice.

When I spoke to Agnes she still hadn't managed to get through to Charles. She would ring me when she had.

I was ravenous. The children had polished off spaghetti hoops but I wanted something more substantial – stir-fried vegetables and rice. I'd just started slicing things up when the phone went. The police?

'Sal, this is Agnes.' She paused.

'Hello. Did you speak to Charles?'

'Dr Goulden is here. I think you better come over. He wants to talk to us.' Her voice sounded strained, shaky. The phone went dead before I could respond.

Ray wasn't back, Sheila was out. I couldn't leave the children and I didn't want to take them with me. I rang Jackie Dobson, whose eldest daughter, Vicky, sometimes babysat. She was saving for a car and every little helped. She was round in five minutes. I asked her to explain to Ray when he got in and I left Agnes' phone number in case there was a crisis. Digger leapt to his feet, inspired by all the rush of activity; was this his big chance?

'No, Digger. You're not coming. Stay.' He slumped. As I left, Maddie and Tom were competing for Vicky's attention by diving off the sofa.

The traffic was snarled up along Wilmslow Road. The delay gave me plenty of opportunity to worry. Goulden must have got

Agnes' address from the phone book, or maybe it was in Lily's notes at Homelea. Presumably he had heard from the police. I wished I'd been able to talk to DS Wignall before I'd set out. Had they actually interviewed Goulden yet? Why did he want to talk to Agnes and me? More threats?

I tapped my fingers on the steering wheel. It was freezing. The heater in the car worked but gave out an ominous stench of burning rubber that caught at the back of my throat. I turned it off. Gazed out at the people walking by: clusters of students in a range of clothing styles – grunge, Joe Bloggs, mod, high street – making their way back from the universities; a large party of women and children in saris and shalwar-kameez, the vivid-coloured, silky material flapping in the wind; an old woman bundled in layers of faded dark clothes peering in a litter bin; a man teetering on the kerb edge, arms wheeling, shouting at the sky.

'Come on,' I muttered. I inched forwards till we reached the junction. The lights were out. A traffic cop was just arriving. Two drivers had managed to collide and were out of their cars, one red-faced, screeching at the other. At last I wheeled right and drove on to Agnes' house. There were no lights on even though the day was fading. There was a Volvo parked directly outside which I assumed was Dr Goulden's. I rang the bell.

He opened the door. Why not Agnes? Half-smile. 'Miss Kilkenny.'

Ms actually.

'Do come in.'

I stepped into the hall, gloomy without the lights on. His bulk made me feel small and vulnerable.

'Where's Agnes?' I demanded.

'We're in the back,' he said.

I headed along to the back room.

'Jesus Christ!'

Agnes sat in her armchair by the gas fire. Her wrists were bound in front of her, her mouth taped up. The creel with its washing lay broken in the corner.

'I had to restrain her.' He spoke calmly. 'She became distressed. I could have used a sedative,' he patted his pocket, 'but she'd have been out for the count. She had the carpet tape out when I arrived.' He motioned to the table where the roll of heavy-duty tape lay.

Agnes' eyes glittered furiously. I was appalled. I turned on him. 'Untie her, now. What the hell do you think you're doing? This is assault. Are you mad? Untie her.'

He made no move. 'We've got to talk,' he said. 'I'm taking you both to the hospital. We need to see Mr Simcock, the consultant. I realise you've had some concerns about Mrs Palmer.' The man was cracked, going on about the need to clear things up while he'd bound and gagged Agnes.

'Untie her,' I insisted.

He looked at me, wearily.

'This is ridiculous. I'm ringing the police.' I snatched up the phone, my heart galloping. The line was dead. He'd ripped out the wires. The realisation brought with it a kaleidoscope of images, mainly from the movies. None of them pretty. A wave of panic. He really was off his trolley. I felt the buzz of fear froth my blood. I relived the endless moment of terror from my past, *waiting for the knife to slide in, watching the blob of spittle dance.*

He smiled thinly. 'The hospital.' He stooped to lift Agnes, his thick, straight blond hair falling forward.

'Wait!' I tried to steady my voice. 'Take those things off her first. We'll come to the hospital but not like that. Untie her.'

'Get on with it.' He brushed past the pair of us and opened the door. I moved to step outside, his arm shot out and he grabbed my hair. Used it to bang my head against

260

the door frame. The sickly pain made me reel, reminding me of childhood falls. His other hand still held the kitchen knife.

Agnes cried out.

'Don't mess me about,' he whispered in my ear. 'You've caused enough trouble, you silly bitch. You, you wait here till she's in the car. You come when I say, understand?'

I did.

He glared at me, considered for a moment. 'If she screams...'

'She won't.'

He twisted round and before I could draw breath yanked the tape from her mouth. Agnes yelped in pain, then pressed her lips together. A band of red bloomed round her mouth where the tape had been.

'Don't!' I swallowed hard. He ignored me. He fumbled with the rough cord around her wrists for a minute before cursing in ex-asperation. He went into the little kitchen, rummaged in a drawer and returned with a small vegetable knife. He sawed at the cord; the knife was sharp and cut through it quickly. Agnes rubbed at her wrists.

'Come on,' he snapped, 'in the car.' He made to take Agnes' elbow but she twisted away and pushed herself to her feet.

'Go on.' He jerked his head. We went

down the hall to the door.

'She'll need her coat,' I said. 'It's freezing out there.'

'Get it,' he hissed at Agnes. She reached for it from the hooks in the hall, put it on, taking her time.

CHAPTER TWENTY-SEVEN

He motioned for Agnes to come and stand in front of him so I could see the knife pointing at her kidneys. 'Don't mess me about,' he repeated.

I stood in the doorway watching as he steered her to the passenger door and into the car. My mind scrabbled for routes of escape but I couldn't come up with anything that wouldn't jeopardise Agnes. At any rate we'd have more chance of attracting attention at the hospital than we would here. I firmly suppressed the idea that Goulden might not be taking us to the hospital once he had us in his car. At least if Ray tried to ring Agnes he'd find the phone wasn't working and realise something was wrong.

He signalled for me to come to the car. I

left the front door slightly ajar – if the wind opened it wider it might alert a neighbour. My legs were unsteady as I walked the few steps to the Volvo. I was at sea and the pavement lurched. I slid into the back seat behind him. The car was impeccable and smelled of some pine air-freshener. Goulden looked into the mirror, his pale blue eyes held mine. I could see he had a large freckle on his lip.

'We're going to the hospital. Don't do anything stupid.' He held up the knife. 'I wouldn't like to have to use this on Mrs Donlan here.'

'Miss Donlan.'

Oh, Agnes. I braced myself but he didn't seem to notice her correction. He used the central locking system to seal us in and started the engine.

We were soon caught up in the traffic jam. I could sense his impatience rising. He began to mutter under his breath, the back of his neck reddened. He put the handbrake on and fished in his pocket for something. Drew out a bottle of tablets, unscrewed the lid and slipped two into his palm. Swallowed them. We crawled forward a few feet. The streetlights came on, red that would soon brighten to orange. A gust of wind spattered rain across the windscreen. I reminded myself to breathe.

What on earth did he intend to discuss with us once he'd got us to the hospital? Did he really think we'd sit down and chat after this violent abduction? We crawled forward a little more. Was Ray back yet? How long before he began to wonder about me, try the number? A siren sounded and gradually an ambulance made its way through the traffic on the other side of the road.

Very slowly I moved my arm and inched my hand towards the door lock. I hadn't a coherent plan in mind but I wanted to see if I could get out of the car if an opportunity arose. I pushed hard with my thumb, praying the lock would move quietly. It wouldn't move at all. Childproof.

The bleeping of the car-phone made me squeal. My hand shot back to my lap. Goulden didn't pick the thing up, just jabbed at it with his fingers.

A woman's voice, cultured, low-pitched. 'Ken, the police have been here asking about the tablets. How the hell did they find out?'

'What did you tell them?' He was anxious.

'I didn't know anything about it. I showed them the records, no entry for that prescription. I told them I'd no idea where they'd come from.'

'They believe you?'

'I don't know. They said they'd want to talk to me again. Oh, Ken, we never should have used Malden's. You should have used a false label, invented a pharmacy.'

Way too late the penny dropped as I recalled the tiny bit of information that Harry had passed on to me: Angela Montgomery was a qualified pharmacist (BPharm, MRPharmS). The letters after her name had meant nothing when Harry had reeled them off. She'd know everything there was to know about making the tablets.

'Bit bloody late for such penetrating insight now, isn't it?' He was scathing.

'If you hadn't lost them none of this—'

'I didn't bloody lose them. Look, I can't talk now.'

'What do you mean? Where are you, Ken? The police want to see you. We need to sort our story out.'

'I know they want to see me,' he spoke through clenched teeth, 'of course they want to see me. I was the prescribing physician, wasn't I? Christ!'

'What are you going to say?'

'Well, if the pharmacy cocks it up, wrong dosage...'

'You don't think they'll believe that?' Her

voice was shrill now. 'They're bound to wonder why you used my lab. They'll keep on snooping and sooner or later they'll start to ask about other things. Don't you see, we have to talk? Come home, I'll meet you there, or here. They won't come back here today. And we need to talk to Matthew. I bet he could come up with something. Tell them it was a blind trial, part of a study.'

'They won't swallow that,' he scoffed.

'Ken, I don't know what to do.' The fight had gone from her. 'I'm scared, come home–'

He cut her off. He took another of his tablets. Then he thumped the steering wheel several times.

At last we reached the main road. He swung on to it, accelerated too fast and had to brake sharply to avoid a cyclist. 'Get off the fucking road,' he cursed. The phone bleeped again, he poked it.

'Ken,' she pleaded, 'don't be like this.'

'Don't be like this.' His mimicry was savage.

'You used me,' she complained.

'Hah!' he snorted. 'That's rich. I used you. You were up to your eyeballs in it, darling, and don't pretend you weren't. You could see Malden's up there with the big boys, couldn't you? Patents left, right and centre. When we

266

found the lesions on this last one you were over the bloody moon. You couldn't wait to get your hands on those tissue samples.' He swerved violently again to avoid a bollard and fell back behind a bus. 'Couldn't wait to get those under your microscope, could you? Well, it's all over now, sweetie – just when we seemed to be getting somewhere, finito.' He cut her off again, gunned the engine and overtook the bus. He caught the wing mirror on the orange and white paint, it bounced back but didn't shatter. I could see Agnes' hand, white knuckles gripping the edge of her seat.

I was uncomfortably aware that we'd been privy to the conversation, as if he didn't care, as if we'd never get the chance to tell anyone about it. I tried to steady my breathing. The worst thing of all would be to panic.

The hospital entrance was in sight. He parked in a reserved bay in the car park near to the entrance. 'You,' he turned to face me, 'you walk beside us. I'll keep this handy.' He showed the knife. Would he have the guts to use it? He had a temper, all right, and he'd not hesitated to smack my head against the door, but would he stab Agnes? It wouldn't be that easy through her clothes. I didn't dare call his bluff yet, but it might come to that.

267

He manoeuvred Agnes in front of him, then let me out. I shivered. I'd been sweating in the car and the cool air chilled me. We went straight in the main entrance, past a security guard who was enjoying a joke with a cleaner. I was praying that our awkward gait and the aura of fear around us might provoke some interest. Nothing. This guard was not the intuitive type. I could sense trouble before I saw or heard it, phero-mones, sixth sense, whatever. I thought it was a fairly universal trait. Obviously it hadn't been on his job description.

'Excuse me,' I called out at exactly the same moment as the two of them erupted with laughter. My voice went unheard. Goulden grabbed my wrist and thrust the knife point into Agnes' clothing. She stiffened.

'All right,' I said. 'Please, don't hurt her.'

Surely we'd meet other people on our way. I was taut with anticipation, waiting for another opportunity. The corridor, so busy by day, echoed with emptiness.

I cast my eyes up to anything resembling a security camera as we made our way down the corridor. Careful to move only my eyes, not my head, so as not to alert Goulden. I tried to reproduce in my eyes the fear that was ricocheting round my belly. Was anyone watching? Were they actually cameras? Was I staring petrified at nothing more than ventilation ducts and junction boxes?

CHAPTER TWENTY-EIGHT

We left the main corridor, turning just past a mosaic depicting a fountain, and headed through some double doors, then another set, into a sort of lobby, low chairs around a table, doors at the far end.

Goulden stopped abruptly at one of the doors. 'Mr Simcock, FRCS' the sign said. He opened the door and snapped on the light. So much for hospital security.

'In here.' He directed Agnes to the far side of the room beyond the large desk. I hovered at the doorway, glancing left and right, memorising the surroundings. 'And you,' he snapped. I stepped into the room.

'Shut the door.'

He picked up the phone on the desk and got through to someone, identified himself and asked whether Mr Simcock were still in the hospital. The reply riled him. 'In theatre? When will he be through?... Well, how long has he been in there? Listen, as soon as he's through I need to see him, matter of urgency. I'm in his rooms. Make sure he gets the message, will you?' They must have agreed, Goulden grunted thanks and replaced the receiver.

'Sit down,' he said to Agnes, pointed at a chair with the knife. Began to dial again.

I was trying to recall the layout outside the room. The lobby with its waiting area had been two sets of double doors from the main corridor. The other way I'd seen another set of swing doors and a fire exit sign. Off the lobby were three or four doors, probably leading to small rooms like this, all on the same side. The best chance would be to head back for the main corridor where there were more likely to be people about. If we went in two different directions Goulden wouldn't know whom to chase. But he still had the knife. He was leaning, half sitting on the desk now and pressing the blade of the knife against the edge, cutting little lines in the wood.

I looked over at Agnes and smiled, be brave. She returned a small smile.

'Douglas? Ken. I'm at the hospital waiting for Matthew. Listen, Angela's had the police over. They've found out about the medication... Eh?...Yes, she died yesterday. Bloody bad luck... No, it was pneumonia, nothing to do with the experiment. But the coroner's requesting a post-mortem. I rang pathology earlier to see when we could collect and they've been told not to release anything. You better get yourself over here...'

He'd sounded fairly collected so far, but Douglas obviously wasn't playing ball. 'Lay low? Christ, they won't leave it now, you know... I don't know what it might "accomplish", maybe bugger all.'

I caught Agnes' attention and with tiny movements of my eyes, fingers and head tried to brief her – you that way, me this. She nodded slowly once. She was game. Now all we needed was a chance.

Disgusted, Goulden began to barrack his brother-in-law. He slid off the desk – it was easier to argue standing up.

'You were more than willing to use the Unit. You supervised the medication there, referred them for scans, lined them up for Matthew. Don't play the innocent.You're up to your ears in this shit, Douglas, and we're all going down together... Of course I can't pull the bloody records... If you get your arse over here maybe between us we can try a bit of damage limitation.' Douglas Mont-

271

gomery's reply didn't please him. He broke the connection. He paced round between Agnes and the window, still keeping an eye on me.

As he turned back and stepped behind the desk I mouthed to Agnes, 'Now!' She was up and out of the chair swiftly. As she moved to the right I lunged for the desk, tipping it right over on to Goulden. I didn't wait to see where he ended up. I scarpered. There was an almighty crash, followed by a roar of outrage. Agnes was heading back towards the main corridor. I went the other way, through the double doors to the fire exit. At the end of the short passageway there was a plain door to the left and the fire door to the right. I hit the bar hard, it shook but the door didn't open. I hit again with the heels of both my hands. It flew open and I lurched forward. There was a rush of cold, damp air, the smell of wet tarmac.

Agnes screamed. My belly jolted in fear. I ran back the way I'd come. Goulden was yanking her back into the office, one arm round her, under her arms, knife in the other fist, kicking at her legs as if she were a life-size puppet.

'Stop it, stop it,' I yelled.

He was shaking her, her head snapping

back and forth.

'Leave her alone, you bastard, let go of her.' I came up behind him. He swung round, threw Agnes from him. For a moment he had a startled, furtive look on his face, it melted and he snarled. I never saw his fist. Just felt it as he belted me square on the nose. The blow knocked me right over. I landed flat on my back, felt the breath punched out of my lungs.

Everything stopped.

I'm going to die, I thought. I've broken my back. There was a peppering of dead flies along the bottom of the fluorescent strip. Oh, God. Maddie. Mum. I was suffocating.

Panic made me gasp, in came the air and with that the pain. Searing, spreading from my nose up behind my eyes. I felt the hot trickle run down the back of my throat, tasted the sweet, iron scent.

I passed out.

I can't have been gone more than a minute and my hearing came back before anything else. A new voice. 'Ken? Good God, man, what on earth's going on? Are you all right, my dear?' The solicitous tone was addressed to Agnes. I don't think he'd spotted me on the floor behind the door. 'You sit down. Was it a fall?'

'Matthew, she's the one, the tablets, she took them, had them sent to a lab.' Goulden spoke quickly, racing to explain. 'The police have been to Malden's. It's only a matter of time.'

I opened my eyes. They hurt, all of me hurt. I could see two pairs of suit trousers, shiny shoes.

'Calm down,' Simcock said coldly. 'What the blazes?' He'd seen me. 'Are you responsible for this?' He flung the words over his shoulder at Goulden as he moved towards me. He was even taller than Goulden but round-shouldered and wiry. With his dark moustache peppered with grey he looked older too.

'They tried to get away. She's the private detective, she got us into this mess. We've got to stop them.'

'You'd better go. You've done enough damage.' The consultant knelt and checked my pulse, used one hand to raise my head and help me up to a sitting position. I leant back against the wall. Put my hand to my face, sticky, swollen. I could see Agnes, she looked dazed, mouth slightly agape, eyes bleary. Had he really hurt her? You could give people brain damage if you shook them too hard, or was that just babies?

274

'Go? Are you off your head? We're in this together, Matthew. Where the hell do you expect me to go?'

'Go home.' He sounded tired. 'I'll get someone to see to you,' he said to me. He moved towards the phone.

'Are you deaf? The police know. They're probably waiting for me there. These two have been on to the coroner, there'll be a full post-mortem. It's all going to come out. They'll want to talk to you and Mont-gomery.'

'I don't know what you're talking about.' There was enough icy fury in the denial to freeze hell but Goulden wasn't cowed. May-be Matthew Simcock just wanted to shut him up or maybe he wanted to save face in front of us. Either way it was too late as far as I was concerned. The phone calls between Dr Goulden, his wife and Douglas Mont-gomery had made it plain that they were all in cahoots. I didn't trust any of them but at least Simcock wasn't beating us up; we'd more chance of leaving here alive now he was here. Meanwhile I'd keep quiet about what we knew and what we suspected.

'Aw, please, spare me,' Goulden retorted. 'I am not carrying the can on my own...'

'You're clearly upset.' Simcock spoke

brusquely. 'I don't know what all this is about—'

'They know!' Goulden blazed. 'Don't bother coming the innocent. These are the bitches that blew the whistle. You haven't got a cat in hell's chance of walking away from this. The police already know I was doping her up to the eyeballs and claiming she had Alzheimer's. Once they get the post-mortem results they'll see there was no haematoma. So they start talking to the theatre staff, they find out we weren't evacuating anything, we were introducing tissue.'

I remembered Simcock's pieces in the Lancet, his pleas for more research into Alzheimer's. Stuff about cloning and bio-genetics and the brain. And all along he'd been busy conducting his very own illicit research programme.

Goulden's face was red with exertion. He lowered his voice, his tone intense and urgent. 'It won't take them long to find out about the others. They'll start looking at the records, uncovering names, five, ten, twenty. All the patients I passed through to Douglas, the ones that came here for scans, the ones with Alzheimer's who so kindly donated their organs. And the ones you operated on, bogus operations, false scan results. All those

276

brains for the research project with Malden's. We are fucked, Matthew.'

'Shut up, you fool, you stupid fool.'

'They know! Don't you?' Goulden jabbed his huge finger at me. 'They bloody know. Tell him.'

Oh God. Did I? Yes? No? What would be the safest reply?

'Lily wasn't senile.' Agnes spoke slowly, I could just hear her. 'You made her act as if she was, with those pills, then you were able to take her to Kingsfield.'

'Weren't they Lily's scans then?' I sounded blurred, like talking after having work at the dentist. Only I hadn't had an anaesthetic before Goulden bashed me. 'He said there were plaques.'

'Yes, there were,' Goulden insisted, 'eventually. But we did it you see, we cultivated the actual, physical changes, the lesions,' he was jubilant now, 'plaques in the hippocampus and in the cortex, clear signs of deterioration.'

'For God's sake!' Simcock tried to silence him but Goulden carried on regardless.

'She was clear as a bell when she moved into Homelea, had her scanned as part of the medical. We induced the disease and for the first time we got over the problem of rejection. A real breakthrough.' He was triumphant.

'Lily didn't fall,' I said. 'She never had any haemorrhage. That was just to cover up what you were really doing, so you could operate.'

'He did a fantastic job,' said Goulden. 'He's one of the best, you know.'

'You're out of your mind!' Simcock exclaimed. He knelt to pick up the phone from where it had fallen. 'I'm ringing security.'

Goulden flew at him. The two men grappled together. It was probably a second or two before it dawned on me that this was the diversion we needed. I rose with effort, feeling giddy.

'Agnes.'

We ran.

CHAPTER TWENTY-NINE

The main corridor was still deserted. We turned left. I saw the fountain mosaic, reassured we were going the right way. There was no one about. Then I heard someone running. Goulden!

Nowhere to hide out here. There was a door to the left. I opened it. A small passageway: two doors along the right-hand wall, a trolley along the left. Nothing else. A dead end. I tried the first door. Locked. The second. Locked. There was an old Tamla song, bright and brassy, something about running and hiding, dancing in lines, with our handbags laid out in front of us. I could feel the pulsing beat as it started ... I heard him getting closer. My heart was thumping. I pulled the trolley towards us, created enough space for us at the far end.

'Get down here, Agnes.'

She moved past me and into the gap. Carefully she edged down into a kneeling position. Hurry up, hurry up. I crouched beside her. The fire door swung open.

I held my breath. Heard his. Panting. How much did the trolley hide? Was he listening? I counted. One, two, like hide and seek but don't giggle, three, no game this, please, help me, please, four, with a cut there is always that delay, the gap between the knife cutting the flesh and the brain realising, sending the messages, admitting the pain, *spittle on his lips...*

The door swung shut.

'Get up!' He leant back, his large frame covering most of the door.

I uncurled, helped Agnes to her feet. Goulden stood, breathing noisily, his head tilted back, hands in his pockets, staring at us through half-closed eyes. We waited. The danger was palpable. Could he smell my fear? Had Tina Achebe waited, cornered like this, time suspended, her senses lucid and singing bright with premonition?

He pushed himself away from the door and moved towards us.

'Wait,' I began, 'can't we just...' God knows what I was going to say, some platitude about talking about things reasonably, I suppose. He came right up close to me, put his hand behind my back. I caught a whiff of his lemony aftershave and the rank odour of sweat. He stepped away suddenly, something white in his hand, not the knife. As he moved I felt the burning sensation. Like a wasp sting. And with it a sense of outrage at being hurt, righteous indignation. Then I panicked. What had he injected me with? A sedative? Something worse? Must ask him. I tried to speak but my tongue was stuck, swelling. Would I die? What a crummy way to die. Tell me. Can't move my lips. Head floating, falling, dissolving.

Cold air. The smell reminded me of school.

Agnes was cradling my head in her lap. That was nice. Her woollen coat was warm on the back of my head and a little itchy on my ear.

'Sal?' A whisper.

I moved to sit up. It was harder than I'd remembered. Everything shook. My muscles hurt, like the flu or the trembly exhaustion after giving birth. My trousers were damp. I must have wet myself.

'Oh, Agnes.'

'Are you all right?'

'I'm not sure.' I was hoarse. I finally got myself into a sitting position. My throat felt as though it had been sandpapered. My tongue was so dry, sore. And my head, there was a piercing pain in my temples.

'Where are we?' I looked around.

'Malden's,' she replied, 'in the warehouse. This is all paper goods.' We were in a large, featureless room. No windows, one door. The walls were lined with shelving which held boxes of paper towels, toilet rolls and the like. Paper and card, the smell of the school store cupboard.

'He drove us here from the hospital,' she said.

'No one stopped him?'

'He put you on that trolley and made me walk next to you. He put on a bedside manner. If anyone had overheard him it would have sounded as if he was taking you to casualty and reassuring me about your condition. He wheeled you all the way to his car.'

'The injection – what was it? How long have I been asleep?'

'I don't know. Some sort of sedative or anaesthetic. I'm afraid I've lost all sense of time. How do you feel?'

'Terrible.' I lifted my hand to my nose, touched it gingerly, the pain made my eyes water.

'Do you think it's broken?'

'I don't know. Oh, I hope not. I don't want to look like a prize-fighter. I'm so thirsty. What about you?'

'I ache a bit,' she smiled.

'Where is he? Is he out there?'

'Yes,' she kept her voice low, 'at least I haven't heard his car drive away. Earlier on I could hear him pacing up and down but it's been quiet for a while.'

I listened. The silence was profound.

'Did he say anything?'

'No. I asked him, when we got here, what he was going to do with us.' Her voice swerved. 'He didn't like me asking. He hurt me.'

'Oh, Agnes,' I scanned her face for bruises, 'are you all right? What did he do?'

'He slapped me, then he kicked me. I expect I've got some pretty colourful bruises but I'm still in one piece.'

'He probably hasn't got a clue what to do with us. He's dug a hole for himself and now he's stuck.'

'If he was going to kill us,' Agnes said, 'he'd have done it by now, wouldn't he?'

At that moment I had total recall of several murder cases where the victims had been held for some time before being killed.

'Hostages,' I said.

'What?'

'Hostages. If we can persuade him that we're more use alive than dead, gives us a chance to build up some relationship with him. But we need to talk to him first.' I made my way quietly over to the door. Peered through the keyhole. It was hard to focus, the pain in my head was pulsing. The space beyond was practically dark. I thought I could make out a figure huddled at the far side but I couldn't be sure. I called his name, banged on the door.

'Dr Goulden, we need to talk. We can

work something out.' I watched through the keyhole. The figure moved. 'The longer this goes on the worse it will be. If you let us go, they'll take that into account.'

'No.' He sounded as though he were in pain too.

'If we can just talk about it...' I carried on. 'After all, it wasn't just you, was it? Simcock played his part, and Montgomery, they ought to take some responsibility too. It just got out of hand, didn't it? The search for a cure?'

'Shut up,' he shouted. 'There's nothing to say. You can't trick me. I'm not stupid.' Suddenly his tone changed, the emotion replaced by a distant practicality. 'It won't hurt. I'm not a cruel man, I get no pleasure from violence. But I need to be careful.' I could hear his footsteps coming closer. 'They have such clever ways these days, don't they, of catching people. But they don't catch all of them. And without evidence, especially without a body, it would be very hard to prove anything.'

I preferred his anger to this quiet, logical reasoning.

'They know you were at Agnes',' I bluffed. 'I told my family when I was leaving that you were there. They're bound to think of you. And what about Simcock? He knows you brought us to the hospital. If you harm us it will make things much worse.'

'No!' He thumped the door. 'I know your game. But it's too late. There's not much time. There's things I need. Yes.'

I heard him move away and shouted after him. 'Dr Goulden, wait, please wait. Let's just talk about it. Dr Goulden.'

I heard the rattling of a corrugated shutter and then more distantly the car engine.

'Now what?' asked Agnes.

I stared back at her, my heart full of dread.

'Now we've got to get out of here.'

CHAPTER THIRTY

'I'll try brute force.' I used the heel of my foot and bashed as near to the lock as I could. Nothing. It looks so easy on the telly but the door wouldn't budge and every time I tried it the throbbing pain in my face made my eyes sting with tears. I lunged again and again, getting more and more desperate, my aim becoming wild with my increasing frustration. My nose started bleeding again. Great crimson splashes on the floor.

'Sal,' Agnes put a restraining hand on my arm, 'it's not working.'

But we'll die, I thought. We can't just wait here for him to come back and slaughter us. Oh God. Maddie and Tom. My stomach twisted with worry. Ray would be back by now. What if Vicky had forgotten to give him Agnes' phone number? I thought of Tina Achebe, of the little terraced house with its Dayglo scene-of-crime tape, of the headlines, photographs, quotes from the neighbours. Which photograph would they use for me?

'It's ridiculous,' I railed. 'We waltzed into the consultant's office at a major hospital with no problems, but getting out of the paper store of a warehouse is like escaping from Alcatraz.' I trembled, swayed against the wall. 'At least I can wipe my nose.' It was a pathetic attempt at humour. Agnes made a pathetic attempt to smile. I found a box of paper towels and pulled some out to staunch the blood.

'Right.' I tried to clear my throat, my voice was getting more and more hoarse. 'We have to work something out for when he comes back.' My heart dipped at the prospect. What chance did we have? A tired old woman and a weak and wobbly younger one. 'He's not going to talk and it's unlikely we could both

286

run away from him. We need to surprise him, stop him for long enough to get help. What have we got that could hurt him?'

We looked at all our potential weapons: car keys, earring wires, Agnes' brooch pin. Weedy or what? There was precious little likelihood of getting near enough to Goulden to plunge a pin accurately into his eyeball or his Adam's apple.

'We need something we can knock him out with,' I said, 'something heavy. Something big so we've more chance of hitting him with it.'

It was bracketed to the far wall. Big, red, shiny and extremely heavy. We debated briefly whether it would be better to spray him with the fire extinguisher or clout him. Clouting had far more going for it.

'The foam might just make him wet. What happens when it's all used up?' I said.

I practised lifting the thing above my head. I remembered log-splitting on some faraway holiday, the stance, the importance of watching the target instead of the tool, the satisfying thwack as the logs split and the shock that rippled back up arms and shoulders if the angle was wrong and the axe bounced off.

We rehearsed our moves. The door opened

inwards to the right. I would stand behind it. We needed to get Goulden into the room far enough for me to move out and take a swing at him. There would only be one chance. If he remained on the threshold it wouldn't work.

'If he does that,' I told Agnes, 'don't leave the room. He can't force you to, not unless he's got a gun. But I don't think he's going to come back with a gun.'

'If he can only see me then he will realise that there's something strange going on, he will know that it is a trap.'

'OK.' I pulled my jacket off. 'Get some paper towels. We'll make a guy.'

Agnes caught on quickly, screwing towel into balls and stuffing them into my jacket. Meanwhile I peeled off my damp trousers and started on them.

'We can use this inside the hood.' She held up a long roll of paper sheeting like they cover examination couches with. She formed it into a big ball for my head. When my dummy was stuffed I dragged boxes of paper off the shelves and constructed a sort of cardboard sofa we could sit on. We arranged the dummy beside Agnes and I surveyed it from the door. It was too obviously not a real person. 'Lie it down, like I was before I came round. That's better. Tuck the feet away. Yes.' The paper face was hidden now and from the door it looked like I was lying prone, pretty much as I had been when I'd regained consciousness.

'When he comes you'll have to say something like I've passed out again or I haven't come round. Something to make him think he's only got one of us to worry about. If he does want us out of here he'll have to carry me out. Tell him you can't wake me.'

There was little else we could do. My stomach was rolling with anticipation. My sweatshirt covered my bottom but I felt exposed as well as cold without my other clothes. There was no heating at all in the room. I'd no intention of losing Agnes, or myself, to hypothermia.

'We must keep warm,' I said. 'Paper's a good insulator. Here, put some of this on your head.' I handed her an armful of the paper sheeting. We both draped our heads. 'Very stylish.' I tore more off to use like shawls. I wrapped sheets around my hips like a skirt. We sat on the sofa.

She adjusted some of the paper sheeting over her legs like a blanket.

'I'm so hungry. I was about to eat when you rang.'

We leant close. I could feel myself warming up where we shared our body heat.

'Somewhere,' she muttered as she fiddled through her coat pockets. 'Aah.' She held out two sweets. 'Barley sugar or Murray mint?'

Oh, Agnes. 'Barley sugar.'

We unwrapped our sweets and sucked.

How long would he be? What things had he gone to get? He'd never let us go now, would he? We knew so much.

'When did you realise,' I asked Agnes, 'that they'd deliberately made Lily demented?'

'Once we knew the high dosages were deliberate. Why else would they do that to her? But I couldn't fathom out what was behind it all. Then when Dr Goulden was talking, I realised there were two lots of patients involved. Remember when you found out what had happened to them, Mr Theakston at Homelea and the other ones from Aspen Lodge, I can't recall all the names.'

'Never mind, it doesn't matter. They all had Alzheimer's, progressive dementia, like the textbooks. All except for Mr Braithwaite, he was a bit different.'

'Yes, and he was the one who had surgery,' she said.

'For the tumour.' I sucked on my sweet, turning it from one cheek to the other.

'They did a biopsy. A bogus operation, like Lily's. And he was on medication,' I pointed out. 'His daughter said something about it.'

'To make him appear senile. He was healthy, he was one of their guinea pigs. Like Lily.'

'Two lots of patients,' I continued piecing it together, 'the healthy ones who were made mad, then operated on, and the others who were the ones who really had Alzheimer's.' I paused. 'Their brains went to Malden's for research. Oh God.' I felt sick. Barley sugar was supposed to be good for travel sickness, but what about other forms of nausea? 'They were using material from those brains. That's what he meant when he said they'd introduced tissue-diseased cells.'

'They can do all sorts, can't they now-adays, clone things, transplant things, use genetic material?' She spoke softly.

'Oh, Agnes, it's horrible.' My mind grappled with the scenario. Everything seemed to fit. 'And if they can develop the disease, they can study it, see how it behaves.'

'That's what they do with animals, isn't it? Grow tumours in mice and monkeys and whatnot.'

'Do you remember when he was talking to his wife, that bit about the drug companies?

That was what they were after. Research that would help them produce a drug. That pathologist I talked to, he said something similar, you'd make millions. Be like inoculations, everyone would want it. Oh, Agnes. Poor Lily.'

'There must have been others too, like Lily and Philip Braithwaite. People they thought no one cared about very much, healthy people getting ill suddenly, having unexpected operations. Lily was their breakthrough, he said, she hadn't rejected the...' She stopped abruptly, emotion taking charge. She snuffled.

'And no one would have been any the wiser if you hadn't been so suspicious.'

'Because we're old, do you see? We're not people, we're pensioners or OAPs,' she stretched the initials out, 'old biddies. No one's surprised if we get demented, it's almost expected.'

'Oh, come on...'

'You'd be surprised.'

'And the donors.' I shivered. 'They were all transferred when they were very ill. Montgomery could send them to Simcock for scans...'

'He would make sure there was plenty of material to harvest,' she said bitterly.

'And once they died the doctors could take the brains, ship them off here, to Malden's. Get the cells they'd cultivate for use on the healthy patients. Yes. And I bet the relatives were only too happy to agree to samples being taken after death, hoping it would help someone in the future.'

I wondered which of the people involved had first come up with the idea for their covert experiments. And why? Had it started off as scientific interest, an altruistic desire to relieve suffering by finding a cure, or-had the prospect of money been the beacon from the start? Had all four of them slept easy in their beds?

My toes had begun to go numb. I circled my ankle, trying to keep the blood moving.

'Are you warm enough?' I asked her.

'Just about.'

'I'm freezing. If only I had a mobile phone we could ring for help.'

'Well, he wouldn't have let you keep it, not if he'd known about it.'

'What happened, before you rang me, when he came to your house?'

She told me how he'd barged in. He'd insisted Agnes ring me. She'd protested it was late but he was emphatic about it. 'I sensed then that it all wasn't as it should be

– the atmosphere more than what he actually said. Then he took me through to the phone. I hoped he'd calm down once I'd made the call but he was so jumpy. He took some of those pills. I asked him to leave and he went completely barmy. Shouting and swearing, he pulled down the old creel, pulled off the rope...'

'Tied you up.' I stretched, the paper rustled, I started on the other ankle. 'It must have been so frightening.'

'And when he pulled the phone out.' She tutted. 'But do you know what went through my mind after fearing for my life? I thought, it's going to cost ever such a lot of money to be reconnected.' She gave a little laugh. 'Isn't that ridiculous?'

I smiled, began writing the alphabet with my foot. 'If we'd only got the results sooner, got on to them sooner...'

'Then maybe Lily wouldn't have died. But we don't know that. You did your best, Sal.'

'But it wasn't enough,' I complained.

'We didn't save Lily but we have found out what's going on. Once we get out of here they'll be stopped, they won't be able to do it to anyone else. They'll be punished.'

'I suppose so. But I am sorry, about Lily.'

CHAPTER THIRTY-ONE

Once we get out of here, she'd said. If we get out of here. How would he try to kill us? Another injection? Did he really think he could get away with it if Agnes disappeared and I did too? There were several people who knew of our recent involvement with him: Moira, for a start, and the police she'd talked to; Matthew Simcock who'd been appalled by Goulden's violence – he'd come forward, surely. Where was Goulden now? On his way back here? He said he'd hide our bodies. How? Bury them? Burn them? Chop them up?

There was silence for a while. The thick walls let little sound in from the outside world. I let my thoughts ramble. People at home would be worried about me. I'd left Agnes' number but no address. How long would they wait until they called the police? And once they did, if they established the address they'd find an empty house and my abandoned car. No indication of where we might be.

How long till morning? Was Maddie fast asleep now or unsettled by the atmosphere as the grown-ups made excuses for my sudden absence?

'You have a daughter?' Agnes asked. Had I been talking aloud?

'Yes, she's five.'

'And you're by yourself?'

'Yes, well, I'm not married. I'm a single parent but we live in a shared house.'

'And the child, she's happy?'

'Yes, I think so. She's never known anything else. She knows families come in lots of different combinations.'

'Times change,' she said, 'and sometimes for the better.'

I waited.

'My sister, Nora, she had a baby. She wasn't married and in those days it was a terrible thing. You were shunned, completely ostracised. There was no mercy.' She smoothed the paper across her knees, running her thumb over creases as she talked.

'Was that before she went to Kingsfield?' I asked.

'That was why she went to Kingsfield. Morally inadequate, they called it. Pregnant and unmarried so they locked her up.'

'Oh God. But your parents...'

'Signed the forms. There was little hesitation. There were many girls like Nora. Young girls. She was only sixteen, little more than a child herself. She had the baby, a little girl, taken from her at birth, taken to be adopted.'

Agnes' niece.

'You never saw the baby?'

'Oh, no. I visited Nora secretly. My mother thought it best to stay away.'

'So Nora stayed there after she'd had the baby?'

'Yes. I don't think they ever said exactly how long she was expected to be there. It was a punishment, you see, rather than treatment. She'd broken the rules. There was no compassion.' She tore a little strip off the edge of her paper sheet and began to roll it into a cylinder in her fingers. 'Nora had been seduced by an older man, a business connection of my father's. He continued to do well.'

'So, they didn't find him guilty of moral inadequacy.'

'Oh, no,' she said ruefully. 'It was cold, very cold, the last time I visited her. There was no snow but one of those easterly winds that cuts right through you. I'd brought her cakes and a ribbon. It was a harsh regime. Most of the girls worked in the laundry, Nora worked in the kitchens.'

Her hand stole to the brooch on her lapel, kneaded at it through the paper, then returned to work at the frills of paper on her lap.

'I arrived just after lunch. They'd finished clearing up. Someone suggested I try the dormitory. She had a bed by the window – huge great windows they had, covered in bars. If she wasn't there I'd put the cakes under her pillow and hope no one stole them. It was quiet up there. The place was deserted.' She cleared her throat.

'Nora was there. She was hanging from the curtain rail. She'd torn her apron into strips and her dress. She just had her shift on. A thin cotton shift. I remember thinking she must be so cold up there, with her poor bare arms, so cold.'

I shivered. I thought of all the mothers' daughters. Nora, whose mother had agreed to her incarceration; Nora's girl child, who would never know the circumstances of her birth; Olive, who had died in infancy and whom Lily had called for in her last waking moments; Tina, whose death had been sudden and brutal. And now in the depth of the night there'd be mothers bearing daughters and daughters mourning mothers, and those railing at each other's shortcomings, and I wanted to be home and warm with my own daughter close by while we still had the chance.

CHAPTER THIRTY-TWO

We talked a lot that night. Agnes told me most of her life story; we made ourselves hungrier fantasising about food. We talked about families, holidays, Manchester, politics, and tentatively about relationships.

'I do get lonely,' I said, 'now and then. I wonder whether I'll ever meet anyone. Wonder if this is it. If it'll feel different the longer I'm on my own.'

'I've been very happy,' she said, 'but then I had Lily.'

I turned to look at her. Her dark eyes were soft, faraway.

I heard the car first. My stomach lurched and I staggered to my feet. 'He's coming.' I wriggled out of the paper that rustled around me and took my position by the door, the fire extinguisher between my feet ready to be lifted. Agnes divested herself of paper and settled the dummy body across her knees. I saw her take a steadying breath. She smiled at me. I swallowed. I could hear the shutter door being unrolled. What if it wasn't Goulden? Perhaps it was the caretaker opening up. Maybe it was morning. My heart leapt with hope. We'd be safe. We could go home.

Footsteps across the concrete floor. My ears were buzzing with the strain of concentration. The scrape of a key in the lock. I could feel my pulse in the roof of my mouth. I prayed, a wordless, soundless plea for help.

The door swung open. Stopped a couple of inches from hitting me. My knees bent, my hands grasped the black handle at the top of the cylinder.

'Get up,' he said quietly.

Come into the room, step forward.

'I can't,' said Agnes, her voice thin and reedy. 'It's Sal, I can't wake her. She's collapsed. I don't know what's wrong.' Her words were laced with panic. I was convinced. But Goulden?

'Christ!' he swore.

'I'm sorry,' Agnes went on, 'I can't lift her. She's too heavy for me. I don't have the strength.'

I heard the tap of his shoe as he stepped

nearer. I swung the extinguisher up and my-self out from behind the door.

He must have caught the movement out of the side of his eye. He wheeled round, in-stinctively lifting his arm to protect himself.

I clung tight to the handle as the cylinder plunged down, the weight was so great I lost control, no opportunity to aim with any accuracy. It skewed to the left, wrenching my wrist. It slammed his arm back and cracked his head. He folded under the impact, tip-ping forward. Blood spurted, from his head, bright, metal-scented. It hit my leg, hot and wet.

I fought the impulse to flee, cut off the growing sense of horror at what I'd done.

He lay face down, arms and legs splayed awkwardly. Blood bubbled out of his head. I pulled my sweatshirt off, bundled it over the crimson fountain. The copious flow made it impossible to see what damage I'd done. Head wounds always bleed a lot, I tried to reassure myself.

Agnes was at my side. I was kneeling in his blood, which was pooling around him, con-gealing quickly in the cold air.

'I'm going to try turning him over,' I said, 'check his breathing. Keep this pressed down.'

She put her hands on the sweatshirt, I arranged his limbs and hauled him on to his back. I bent low, my ear by his mouth and nose listening, my eyes watching his chest for motion. It was hard to tell. I turned my head to look at him. His eyes flew open and his hand grabbed my throat. I screamed and scrabbled to get away, clawing at his hand with my own. His grip weakened and I pulled free. I scrambled to my feet, slipped in his blood and nearly fell on him. I regained my balance and fought to slow my breathing. His eyes were shut again.

I struggled to remember first aid. There was something about raising the wound above the heart – or was that only legs and arms? 'I'll go for help,' I said. 'Here,' I pulled my jacket from the dummy and fashioned a cushion, 'lift his head, put this underneath. Will you be all right?'

Agnes nodded, her face was blank with shock. 'Go on,' she said.

It didn't take me long to establish that there were no offices in the warehouse, no phones. Outside dawn was breaking, the light hurt my eyes. I could see Goulden's car and across the yard the main building. Steel shutters covered all the doors and windows. No one was at work yet. There was a heavy dew, the world was soaked and there was a powerful smell of fertiliser.

It was hard to think straight. Where could I get help? Looking about I could see fields, trees and pylons but no other buildings. The land was flat, the sky dominating most of the view, grey to the east where the day was beginning but still dark behind me. I listened for traffic. I thought I could make out a distant drone but I couldn't tell if it was in my head or out there.

If I'd had my wits about me I might have taken his car or used his car-phone to summon help but I'd lost all sense somewhere in the fear and the bleeding, and the only thing that occurred to me was to walk until I found someone.

I set off jogging slowly down the narrow road that led to Malden's. It was laid with white gravel, like the stones that Hansel dropped. I wanted to lie down and sleep. I wanted to hide somewhere far away where they'd never find me.

Guilt. Fear. Had Tina Achebe's killer felt it? Had he been drenched in blood. Beaten to death she'd been, how many blows? She was a tiny woman, nothing like Goulden with his broad shoulders, his big bones. Had Tina's murderer used a weapon or just his fists? There'd never been anything in the papers about a weapon. Had her head burst like Goulden's?

To the rhythm of my steps I chanted a mantra: *Don't let him die, please, don't let him die.* He may have been a grade A dickhead but I didn't want to be his murderer.

The road led to a T-junction. A quaint black and white signpost told me that I was five miles from Northwich and one and a half from Little Leigh. One and a half. Waves of pity nudged me. It wasn't fair. How could I walk another mile and a half? I was tired and thirsty. So thirsty. I had a sudden vivid memory from childhood, morning walk to school, trailing my fingers through the privet hedges sucking dew from my fingertips.

I stepped up to the hedge. Full of hawthorn and brambles. I felt like throwing a tantrum. There was a little grass growing beneath the hedge. I ran my hands through a clump, washing away the worst of the rusty blood-stains. Then I found a fresh patch and ran my hands through it, licking the droplets of dew from my palms and fingers. There was a large spider's web in the hedge, strung with silver beads of dew, diamonds. Perfect. I got to my feet shivering. Aware again of how weak I felt, how much I ached. A mile and a half then.

I pushed myself again, tried to establish a rhythm, the air in my windpipe burning with each gasp. *Please don't let him die, please, don't let him die.* I could taste my lungs. Past the tall tree on the left. Cows to the right, huge Friesians, like cartoons, black and white against the lush grass. Another gate. Please don't let him die.

Then I saw the man and his dog.

There's always a man and a dog, isn't there? While the rest of us luxuriate in the final hour in bed the dog walkers are up and out, rain or shine, discovering the dark deeds the night has spawned. Stumbling over shallow graves, corpses.

He was a small man, middle-aged, glasses and a neat moustache. He wore a waterproof jacket and a woolly hat. He looked shocked when he first saw me, then concerned as we drew closer. You couldn't blame him. Clad in a T-shirt, smashed-up face, spattered red. The dog was small, brown, nondescript, friendly enough. It tried to lick the blood off my leg.

'Get an ambulance,' I said to the man, 'and the police.'

'Has there been an accident? Are you all right?' He pushed the dog away from me gently with his foot. 'Get down, Shep.'

Shep! I felt a giggle inflate in my belly.

305

'Yes, please hurry. Tell them there's a man with head injuries, up at Malden's, you know where...'

He nodded. 'Come on, Shep.' He began to run, really run, the dog at his heels. I turned back for Malden's.

Above me I heard the roar of a plane ascending from the airport. The sky was too cloudy to see it but I could hear it climbing. Full of passengers bound for sunny holidays. Up for hours already, they'd have been. Stomachs sour with lack of sleep and food at funny times, wondering whether to risk the curdled eggs and the strange sausages on the in-flight meal.

I leant over the road and retched. Thin, foamy bile.

Don't let him die.

CHAPTER THIRTY-THREE

Agnes was still beside him, pressing my sweatshirt to his head. He was still breathing, just. I sat beside her, told her help was on its way. I closed my eyes and waited.

A second ambulance was summoned by

the first. Goulden was given immediate emergency treatment before being moved. The police took initial statements from us. The bare bones of the story that had brought us here, leaving us shocked and bloodied. We were wrapped in blankets and led blinking into the bright daylight to the ambulance.

At the casualty department people came and went checking pulse and temperature. They let me ring home. Ray answered, relief catching at his voice. I told him where I was and that I'd be home as soon as they'd checked me out. I didn't tell him what had happened. I wasn't sure. Had I killed a man? Brain-damaged him?

I couldn't get warm. They took my clothes and left me a paper gown which was open at the back and one cellular blanket. I asked for more blankets. They never came. There weren't even any rolls of paper sheeting I could make use of. We were waiting again, for an X-ray, for a doctor, for a diagnosis, for ever. Shock dulled my comprehension but I didn't dare sleep.

At last someone offered us tea. Oh, yes, yes! When it arrived, pale grey in Styrofoam cups, I nearly wept with disappointment. It didn't even seem to help my raging thirst. More police came. They spoke to Agnes and me together.

They managed to note down the main points of our story and our conspiracy theory without too many incredulous looks. I asked about Goulden. He'd been taken to another hospital; there were no intensive care beds free at this one. They didn't know how he was.

The doctor checked us over, pronounced our X-rays clear and agreed we could be discharged. They cleaned us up first. They decorated my nose with steri-strips, which looked stupid, and strapped up my wrist. Agnes had badly bruised legs from the kicking she'd received. They dressed them for her. We were both given some painkillers to take with us, a poorly photocopied leaflet on hypothermia, shock and concussion and what to look out for, and our choice of old clothes from the Hospital Friends Box. I was going to ask about my own clothes until I realised with a rush of fear that they might constitute evidence of my assault on Goulden. Did they need evidence when I'd told them all about it?

It was well after lunchtime when we were escorted to Agnes' house in a police car. I insisted that someone go in with Agnes and check it out.

'I'll be fine,' she said.

'Your phone's cut off,' I said. 'Your door was open half the night, anyone could have been in.'

'It's best we check it out, madam,' said the driver, and he and his partner got out.

'I'll ring BT,' I said, 'order a repair.'

'No,' she objected.

'It's no trouble.'

'Sal, I'm perfectly capable of going next door to use my neighbour's phone to do that. I don't need looking after,' she admonished me.

'Sorry.' I made a note of the neighbour's number in case I needed to contact Agnes, and the police did the same when they returned and pronounced the house secure. She watched us go from the doorstep. I turned to keep her in view as long as possible. I had an urge to run back and stay with her. Agnes and I, we'd been somewhere terrible together; no one else could ever really know what it had been like. And we'd survived. I took a deep breath and sat back in my seat.

CHAPTER THIRTY-FOUR

Digger was inordinately pleased to see me. Made me feel guilty as hell seeing I have so little regard for the animal. Still, unrequited love doesn't seem to faze him.

Ray paled when he saw me and he fussed round me until I gave him something to do. 'Ray, please, I want a pot of tea, strong. And porridge, loads, with golden syrup.'

'I know how you take your tea,' he retorted.

He'd contacted the police when I'd failed to return. The police had found my car but had not got any further in their efforts to find me.

Sheila arrived back from lectures as I was eating the first mouthful. 'Oh, you poor thing. Is it broken?'

'No, just bruised.'

'You've got black eyes.'

'No,' said Ray, 'more like purple. Prettier than last time.' He put down my tea, pulled out a chair.

'Has this happened before?' Sheila was aghast.

'No,' I said.

'Yes,' said Ray.

'That was a gun,' I said, 'this was a fist.'

'You were hurt,' he raised his voice, 'you were hurt then and you're hurt now.'

'I know. Don't shout at me. I don't like being hurt, I don't try to get hurt. It frightens me too.'

For a beat or two the unspoken argument hung in the air. We'd been through it before. Ray would never like the risks the job brought with it and would never understand why I persisted in it. But I loved my work. In spite of the bad breaks and the dull days there was nothing else I could imagine being halfway happy doing.

'Right,' he said. 'Let's have it.'

'What?' I swallowed a mouthful of tea, then another. Bliss.

'From start to finish. I've been up all night worried sick, talking to police, trying to convince them I wasn't being neurotic, covering for you with the kids, imagining you floating down the Mersey or crumpled into a wheelie bin somewhere. The very least I expect is a blow-by-blow account of what's been going on.'

He got it. Sheila too. And the telling of it helped relieve me of some of the awful tension that had my shoulders up near my earholes and my guts like macrame. They were suitably appalled at the central image of people being given diseased brain matter as a means of pushing forward the search for a cure for Alzheimer's. I finished with an account of our planned attack on Goulden.

'I ran out and found a man walking his dog. He called an ambulance. I still don't know how Goulden is. They took him to intensive care in Chester.'

Sheila swallowed and Ray was quiet, lost for words. I couldn't deal with their shock as well as my own.

I pushed back my chair and got up. 'I must have a bath.'

I pushed Blu-Tack into the overflow and filled the bath, dripped in some geranium and rose oils. I found one of my old Marvin Gaye tapes and put it on. My face was a mess, nose still swollen and mottled, lips cracked, eyes bleary and bruised. The ridiculous lattice of steri-strips contrasted vividly with the bruised plum background.

Marvin sang about injustice and love and loss. The bathroom filled with steam, which condensed on the mirror and the walls and dribbled down the tiles.

Drops leaked down my face too but they were salty and of my own making.

I had barely half an hour before the children would be home. I craved sleep but wanted to see Maddie first, reassure her all was well. I'd already agreed with Ray and Sheila that as far as the kids were concerned we should say I'd been hit by a baddie and the police were going to put him in jail.

'Are they?' Sheila had asked. 'If he's all right?'

'Bloody hope so. I don't know what the charges will be, aggravated assault, conspiracy, abduction, maybe even manslaughter as far as the deaths of some of those patients go. They can take their pick.'

I wrapped my big old coat round me and sat outside in the garden while I waited. There was a watery sun reflecting softly off the drops on the leaves and grass. Everything was damp and a bit grey round the edges but there were a few signs of the summer to come: shiny curled shoots on the clematis round the back door, buds and bright new leaves on the aubretia. I felt melancholy. The violence had made its mark inside as well as on the surface. I felt weepy and burdened down. Recognised once again the huge gap

313

between the world I wanted and the one I was living in. I'd failed Agnes and Lily. There was little consolation in the knowledge that I'd been able to stop Goulden killing us.

I needn't have worried about Maddie. Once she'd established that I wasn't dying and had enjoyed a good tour of my injuries she lost interest. I enquired about school. It was boring.

'What's boring?'

'All of it.'

'What did you do?'

'Nothing.' She was growing impatient.

I could remember the same inquisition from my own mother, though at a later age. I'd always fobbed her off with the details of the school dinner menu, not an option if you took packed lunches as Maddie did. I could never comprehend why she had any interest in what I did in those long tedious lessons. Why then, if I could remember what it was like, did I persist in asking Maddie the same questions?

'You must have done something.'

'Fish,' she said enigmatically. And that was the end of the matter.

The phone rang. It was one of the police officers to tell me that Goulden was out of the woods and the prognosis was good. They'd found ropes, drugs and weights in his car, plenty to substantiate our belief that he intended to murder us. His wife would be helping them with their enquiries, as would her brother. They were looking for Matthew Simcock. I thanked him profusely for letting me know. I'd worked on cases before where getting any such information was like drawing teeth. There was no obligation to tell victims what was happening to villains. I asked him to make sure Agnes knew too.

The relief made me dizzy. I'd been frightened silly that Goulden would die, that I'd have a man's life on my conscience. I sat on the bottom stair. I felt a flare of anger then. Searing hot, in my guts, up my spine, pricking my eyes. Rage at what Goulden had done to me, to Agnes, to Lily. A blaze of fury that I hadn't dared to allow whilst his life hung in the balance. It felt good, burning up some of the guilt and the self-blame. Slowly it ebbed away. I was too drained to sustain it. Ray found me gazing into the middle distance.

'Go to bed,' he said.

'Yeah, I will.' I said goodnight to the children. Hugged them both tight.

'You're going to bed before me!' Maddie was delighted.

'I know. I'm so tired. If I don't get some sleep I'm going to fall over.'

'You're not,' she scoffed. 'I know! I can put you to bed.'

I allowed her to burble round me while I got myself undressed and into bed. I took some more paracetamol and wriggled under the duvet. 'Night-night.' I leant out of the side to kiss her on the head. 'I love you, Maddie.'

'Mummy?'

'What?'

'My nose is a bit sore too, on the inside. You can't see it on mine.'

'Well, there's not a lot you can do about that, Maddie.'

'A plaster might help.'

'Not on the inside.'

'No, outside.'

'Fine.' All I wanted to do was sleep. 'They're in the kitchen. Tell Ray I said you could have one. Night-night.'

'And cream.'

'Yep.'

'I might need two plasters, you know.'

Irritation rose like bile, but I tried to keep it from my voice. 'Fine.' You can use the whole bloody box as long as you let me sleep.

I awoke aching and disoriented at midnight. My throat was parched, my head thumped with pain, my nose was blocked. I didn't dare blow it. I crept downstairs and made tea and toast with lashings of honey. Sat in my old armchair in the kitchen to eat it. Digger padded over and laid his head on my foot. Nice gesture, spoilt a bit by the drool. I gently pushed him away.

Matthew Simcock committed suicide. He was found that morning in his car, up near Snake Pass. There's a viewing point where you can see right across the tops. He'd attached a tube to the exhaust. It's a beautiful spot, the bright grass of the peaks and the white limestone walls. His death made the late editions. There was no mention then of the background, just the bald facts.

The jury found Bill Sherwin not guilty of murdering Tina Achebe. The case had received quite a lot of local coverage but all the evidence was circumstantial, there was no witness, no forensic or other proof that Mr Sherwin had even been to Levenshulme that morning. The prosecution claimed that Tina had tried to end the relationship and that the murder had been the act of a jilted lover. The jury weren't convinced. The judge made acerbic comments about excessive zeal and inadequate preparation of the prosecution case.

Diane's exhibition was a big success. The haircuts were out in force. Shortly after it closed she took me with her on a shopping expedition. She was going to treat herself to a real fire, she'd had the chimney opened up and now needed a proper fire surround. She was after an antique, something with painted tiles.

Parking near the antique hypermarket was difficult. I found a space in a side street close to the road where the Achebes had lived. There was a yard halfway down, a dairy, busy with lorries and floats, a public phone box opposite. I parked nearby. As we got out I heard the familiar squawk of a Tannoy above the roar of a truck.

And my heart stood still.

The publishers hope that this book has given you enjoyable reading. Large Print Books are especially designed to be as easy to see and hold as possible. If you wish a complete list of our books please ask at your local library or write directly to:

Magna Large Print Books
Magna House, Long Preston,
Skipton, North Yorkshire.
BD23 4ND

This Large Print Book, for people
who cannot read normal print,
is published under the auspices of

THE ULVERSCROFT FOUNDATION